阅读·思维训练教程

Thinking Through Reading

赵明学　编著

内容提要

这是一本以丰富学生的思想、开展思维训练和培养思辨能力为目的的英语阅读教材。既通过阅读，接触不同思想，引导学生进行独立思考，然后通过师生以及学生间的互动交流，达到丰富学生的思想内涵，提升学生的思辨能力，养成良好思维习惯的教学目的。

责任编辑：王辉

图书在版编目(CIP)数据

阅读·思维训练教程/赵明学编著. —北京：知识产权出版社，2010.9

ISBN 978-7-5130-0577-7

Ⅰ.①阅… Ⅱ.①赵… Ⅲ.①英语—阅读教学—高等学校—教材 Ⅳ.①H319.4

中国版本图书馆CIP数据核字(2011)第091226号

阅读·思维训练教程/Thinking Through Reading

YUE DU · SI WEI XUN LIAN JIAO CHENG

赵明学　编著

出版发行：知识产权出版社

社　址：	北京市海淀区马甸南村1号	邮　编：	100088
网　址：	http://www.ipph.cn	邮　箱：	bjb@cnipr.com
发行电话：	010-82000893　82000860转8101	传　真：	010-82000893
责编电话：	010-82000860-8129	责编邮箱：	wanghui@cnipr.com
印　刷：	保定市中画美凯印刷有限公司	经　销：	新华书店及相关销售网点
开　本：	787mm×1092mm　1/16	印　张：	11.25
版　次：	2011年9月第1版	印　次：	2011年9月第1次印刷
字　数：	200千字	定　价：	36.00元

ISBN 978-7-5130-0577-7/H·059(3474)

前　言

阅读，是一个获取知识的过程，是通往博学多识的必由之路。鲁迅先生晚年病重时表示：“倘能生存，我仍要学习。”“删夷枝叶的人，决定得不到花果。”

阅读，是一个开阔胸襟视野的过程。若要如此，就要放开度量，大胆地，无畏地，尽量地吸收古今中外的文化知识。不容纳百川，无以汇成大海。

阅读，是一个思考、探索的过程。思索不是一种苦思冥想的活动，而是把所读内容同客观现实联系起来，加以观察，内省外思，取精用宏。“学而不思则罔。”

阅读，是一个比较鉴别的过程。为了比较，就要敢于接触不同的观点，看看为自己所不解或反对的人和事究竟是怎样的，凡真伪、是非、优劣，都可以通过比较得到鉴别。“多闻择其善而从之。”

阅读，是对思维能力的培养和心智机制的训练。理解能力，记忆能力，综合的能力，分析的能力，判断的能力，想象的能力，感悟和体验的能力等都可以从中受惠。阅读是可以培养能力的，当思想得以飞跃，情绪得以激昂，“创新”还会无动于衷吗？至此，阅读才走过“学—思—行”的全程。“我思，故我在。”

阅读，何尝不可以是一种“享受”呢？当你为某人的精神而叹服；当你为某人的真实所感动；当你的思想因和某人的对话而自由驰骋；当你为和某人笔下的那些美丽天使的舞姿而欢娱；等等。享受，是阅读过程中的一种身心状态。当你读出一个“自我”，阅读活动就回归了“人本”。

就语言而言，不外乎涉及语言形式和语言所表达的思想内容两个方面。思想需要语言这一表现形式；而文字如果没了思想内容，至多是一种书法艺术。对于一个人来说，道理相同。

带着以上对阅读的认识,我编著了这本《阅读·思维训练教程》。其实,“reading for thinking”和“reading for being”更能真正代表我编写此书的心思。前者是方法,后者是目标,即以期通过“阅读与思考”这样一种大脑训练方式,使大家养成思考的习惯,丰富思想内涵,培养思辨能力,深刻挖掘自我,为全面提升“人”这个 being 的品质,投注一臂之力。

全书共选文 16 篇,为利于阅读理解,有的选文作了部分删改;练习的设计和编写全部是为 reading for thinking 这一思维训练目的服务的。

编者

2011 年 8 月

TABLE OF CONTENTS

Passage 1

OPEN YOUR MIND

1 In most modern bookshops there is a large section devoted to business and how to succeed in it. Many of these books talk about particular problems, like how to manage time or motivate staff. Others are written by successful entrepreneurs who want to tell the public how they build their businesses. Now there is also an increasing number of books telling us how to use the most valuable resource in the world. That is the human brain.

2 The science of psychology was developed by doctors who wanted to treat the causes of mental illness. It was not long before people realized that the study of the mind could also be used to help healthy brains work better. This process could then be applied to business. As far back as the 1920s, people who wanted to succeed were urged to "think and grow rich". Another technique was to say "Everyday and in every way I will become better and better" before going to bed at night.

3 Since those days we have learned far more about how the brain actually works. One of the most surprising facts is that it hardly works at all. On average, people only use 1% of their brain power in everyday life. It is as though we have inherited a huge mansion and decided to live in the bathroom. How can we explore the other rooms, make ourselves at home and take full possession of our thinking processes?

4 Psychologists have come up with a number of answers that can be applied to our daily work and life. Some of these encourage us to expand our brain power. Speed-reading, for instance, is a way of training people to understand words in groups rather than individually.

5 Other techniques encourage us to change the way we think. "Lateral Thinking", for instance, encourages us to solve problems by looking at them in many different ways and exploring every possibility which might provide a solution. "Brainstorming" is a way of generating ideas by discussion. The views of one speaker produce ideas in other members of the group.

6 Another technique, "Mind Mapping", encourages people to visualize situations in pictures rather than in words. In this way we can look at things as a whole rather than focusing on individual activities. We can then identify problems that might occur, in advance, rather than dealing with things as they happen.

7 What all of these ideas have in common is that they attempt to solve problems through creativity. They are based on the discovery that different parts of the brain control different areas of our thinking process. The left side of the brain controls logic and learning. The right side controls our imagination and our artistic sense.

8 Traditionally, education and working life have emphasized the left brain over the right. Knowledge and rational thinking are regarded as better guides than imagination. Traditional thought says that it is better to learn what everybody else knows than to think differently. In reality this approach to life makes things more difficult. Both sides of our brain are meant to be used together, just as we use both hands to tie our shoelaces.

9 If we are given a choice between two things that work equally well we will always choose the most beautiful. This fact shows the influence of our right brain and explains why design is now a vital part of business thinking. Industrial designer Frank Nuovo recently described how he deliberately appealed to the creative instinct. "I want to create something that would make people reach out and say 'I like this'.

10 In the past, businesses and other large organizations have tended to create a "culture of conformity". Individuality and creativity were discouraged. Now many are learning that this is a mistake. At every level, the future belongs to those who can dream.

WORDS AND PHRASES

conformity[kən'fɔːməti] *n.*	behavior that follows accepted rules
inherit[in'herit] *v.*	receive property or money from someone after they have died
instinct['instiŋkt] *n.*	a natural feeling, knowledge, or power
lateral['lætərəl] *adj.*	of or at the side
make oneself at home	be comfortable with one's surroundings
mansion['mænʃən] *n.*	a very large house

I. Understanding the Text

◇ *Understand the subject matter.*

◇ *Read for the main information.*

◇ *Learn the writing technique.*

◇ *Reach the conclusion.*

1. What is the theme of the passage?

____

2. What are the main points made in this passage?

Para. 1 – 2: ______________________________

Para. 3 – 6: ______________________________

Para. 7: ______________________________

Para. 8 – 9: ______________________________

Para. 10: ______________________________

3. What is the conclusion drawn in this passage? (Para. 10)

____

II. Analyzing the Paragraphs

◇ *Summarize the information.*

◇ *Generalize the main idea.*

◇ *Find out the topic sentence.*

1. What is the main idea of Paragraph 1?

____

2. What is the main idea of Paragraph 2?

____

3. What is the main idea of Paragraph 3?

____

4. What is the main idea of Paragraph 4?

____

5. What is the main idea of Paragraph 5?

____

6. What is the main idea of Paragraph 6?

____

7. What is the main idea of Paragraph 7?

____

8. What is the main idea of Paragraph 8 and 9?

____

9. What is the main idea of Paragraph 10?

____

III. Learning the Language

◇ *Be aware of and sensitive to language variations and varieties.*

◇ *Choose the language as being used in the passage.*

◇ *Learn the best language.*

1. In most modern bookshops there is a large ________ devoted to business and how to succeed in it. (Para. 1)

   A) section　　B) part　　C) counter　　D) place

2. Others(books) are written by successful entrepreneurs who want to tell the public how they ________ their businesses. (Para. 1)
   A) build B) make C) establish D) create
3. Now there is also a(n) ________ number of books telling us how to use the most valuable resource in the world. (Para. 1)
   A) much B) many C) increasing D) increased
4. Since those days we have learned far more about how the brain actually works. One of the most surprising facts is that it hardly ________ at all. (Para. 3)
   A) functions B) works C) operates D) starts
5. How can we explore the other rooms, ________ and take full possession of our thinking processes? (Para. 3)
   A) let ourselves at home B) make ourselves at home
   C) allow ourselves at home D) comfort ourselves at home
6. On average, people ________ 1% of their brain power in everyday life. (Para. 3)
   A) only use B) use only C) only take D) take only
7. Psychologists have ________ a number of answers that can be applied to our daily work and life. (Para. 4)
   A) taken up with B) got up with
   C) brought up with D) come up with
8. "Brainstorming" is a way of ________ ideas by discussion. (Para. 5)
   A) producing B) making
   C) constructing D) generating
9. Both sides of our brain are meant to be used together, just as we use both hands ________ our shoelaces. (Para. 8)
   A) to tie B) to fasten C) to knot D) to secure
10. Industrial designer Frank Nuovo recently described how he deliberately appealed to the creative ________. (Para. 9)
   A) instinct B) distinct C) extinct D) distinct

IV. Thinking Openly

◇ *Keep your mind open to new ideas.*

◇ *Be receptive to other's opinions.*

◇ *Challenge your own judgment.*

1. The most valuable resource in the world is the human brain. (Para. 1)
   What do you think?

   ____

   ____

2. On average, people only use 1% of their brain power. (Para. 3)
   What do you want to say after reading this statement?

   ____

   ____

3. Speed-reading is a way to expand our brain power. (Para. 4)
   How do you explain this?

   ____

   ____

4. Brainstorming is a way of generating ideas by discussion. (Para. 5)
   What can you learn from this statement?

   ____

   ____

5. The left side of the brain controls logic and learning. The right side controls our imagination and our artistic sense. What comes to your mind with this information? (Para. 7)

   ____

   ____

6. Traditionally, education and working life have emphasized the left brain over the right. (Para. 8) Is this generally true in China's education?

   ____

   ____

V. Thinking Critically

◇ *Be critical in your thinking.*

◇ *Be skeptical in your thinking.*

◇ *Be introspective in your thinking.*

1. How many ways of thinking can you come up with?

2. What is/are the way(s) of thinking you most frequently use?

3. How can 'speed-reading' be a way of expanding our brain power?

4. What is 'lateral thinking'?

5. Is 'brain storming' a way of your generating ideas?

6. Which is more important? To learn what everybody else knows or to learn to think differently.

7. The point(s) that I do not agree with the writer.

VI. Thinking Independently

◇ *Develop and form ideas or opinions of your own.*

◇ *Be both inductive and deductive in your thinking.*

◇ *Communicate and share with others.*

◇ *Write and present your composition on one of the following topics.*

1. How to open one's mind
2. My way of opening my mind
3. The potentials of human mind
4. The importance of developing our thinking ability
5. Living in the "bathroom" or in the "huge mansion"
6. One thing I have learned from this passage

Passage 2

GIVE US 15 MINUTES A DAY

1 Your boss has a bigger vocabulary than you have. That's one good reason why he's your boss. This discovery has been made in the word laboratories of the world. Not by theoretical English professors, but by practical, hard-headed scholars who have been searching for the secrets of success.

2 After a host of experiments and years of testing they have found out: That if your vocabulary is limited your chances of success are limited. That one of the easiest and quickest ways to get ahead is by consciously building up your knowledge of words. That the vocabulary of the average person almost stops growing by the middle twenties. And that from then on it is necessary to have an intelligent plan if progress is to be made. No haphazard hit-or-miss methods will do.

3 It has long since been satisfactorily established that a high executive does not have a large vocabulary merely because of the opportunities of his position. That would be putting the cart before the horse. Quite the reverse is true. His skill in words was a tremendous help in getting him his job.

4 Dr. Johnson O'Connor of the Human Engineering Laboratory of Boston and of the Stevens Institute of Technology in Hoboken, New Jersey, gave

a vocabulary test to 100 young men who were studying to be industrial executives.

5 Five years later those who had passed in the upper ten percent all, without exception, had executive positions, while not a single young man of the lower twenty-five percent had become an executive.

6 You see, there are certain factors in success that can be measured as scientifically as the contents of a test-tube, and it has been discovered that the most common characteristic of outstanding success is "an extensive knowledge of the exact meaning of English words."

7 The extent of your vocabulary indicates the degree of your intelligence. Your brain power will increase as you learn to know more words. Here's the proof.

8 Two classes in a high school were selected for an experiment. Their ages and their environment were the same. Each class represented an identical cross-section of the community. One, the control class, took the normal courses. The other class was given special vocabulary training. At the end of the period the marks of the latter class surpassed those of the control group, not only in English, but in every subject, including mathematics and the sciences.

9 Similarly it has been found by Professor Lewis M. Terman, of Stanford University, that a vocabulary test is as accurate a measure of intelligence as any three units of the standard and accepted Stanford-Binet I. Q. tests.

10 The study of words is not merely something that has to do with literature. Words are your tools of thought. You can't even think at all without them. Try it. If you are planning to go down town this afternoon you will find that you are saying to yourself: "I think I will go down town this afternoon." You can't make such a simple decision as this without using words. Without words you could make no decisions and form no judgments whatsoever.

11 A pianist may have the most beautiful tunes in his head, but if he had only five keys on his piano he would never get more than a fraction of

these tunes out. Your words are your keys for your thoughts. And the more words you have at your command, the deeper, clearer and more accurate will be your thinking.

12 A command of English will not only improve the processes of your mind. It will give you assurance; build your self-confidence; lend color to your personality; increase your popularity. Your words are your personality. Your vocabulary is you.

13 Your words are all that we, your friends, have to know and judge you by. You have no other medium for telling us your thoughts—for convincing us, persuading us, giving us orders.

14 Words are explosive. Phrases are packed with TNT. A simple word can destroy a friendship and land a large order. The proper phrases in the mouths of clerks have quadrupled the sales of a department store. The wrong words used by a campaign orator have lost an election. For instance, on one occasion the four unfortunate words, "Rum, Romanism and Rebellion"[1] used in a Republican campaign speech threw the Catholic vote and the presidential victory to Grover Cleveland.[2] Wars are won by words. Soldiers fight for a phrase. "Make the world safe for Democracy." "All out for England." "V for victory." The "Remember the Maine" of Spanish War days has now been changed to "Remember Pearl Harbor."

15 Words have changed the direction of history. Words can also change the direction of your life. They have often raised a man from mediocrity to success.

16 If you consciously increase your vocabulary you will unconsciously raise yourself to a more important station in life, and the new and higher position you have won will, in turn, give you a better opportunity for further enriching your vocabulary. It is a beautiful and successful cycle.

17 For words can make you great!

(By *Wilfred Funk* and *Norman Lewis*)

Notes on the Text

[1] "Rum, Romanism and Rebellion"

In the 1884 presidential campaign, the Republic candidate James G. Blaine had originally a strong following among the Irish-Americans, most of whom were Catholics. But when Burchard, a supporter of Blaine' made a campaign speech in which he described the Democratic Party as a party of "Rum(郎姆酒), Romanism(天主教), and Rebellion," Blaine neglected to rebuke this insult to the faith of his Irish American followers, thus losing their vote.

[2] Grover Cleveland(1837-1908): the 22nd(1885 – 1889) and 24th (1893 – 1897) President of the United States.

WORDS AND PHRASES

a host of	a large number of
at one's command	ready to be used
control class	(做实验)对照班
cross-section	a representative example of the whole
fraction【ˈfrækʃən】*n.*	a small part
haphazard【hæpˈhæzəd】*adj.*	not planned
hard-headed *adj.*	shrewd and unsentimental
identical【aiˈdentikəl】*adj.*	exactly equal/alike
mediocrity【ˌmiːdiˈɔkrəti】*n.*	the state of being neither very good nor very bad
orator【ˈɔrətə】*n.*	a person skilled in public speaking
put the cart before the horse	do things in the wrong order
quadruple【ˈkwɔdrupl】*v.*	increase by four times

I. Understanding the Text

◇ *Understand the subject matter.*

◇ *Read for the main information.*

◇ *Learn the writing technique.*

◇ *Reach the conclusion.*

1. What is the theme of this passage?

____

2. What are the main points made in this passage?

Para. 1 – 6: ______________________________

Para. 7 – 9: ______________________________

Para. 10 – 11: ______________________________

Para. 12 – 13: ______________________________

Para. 14 – 15: ______________________________

3. What is the conclusion drawn in this passage?

Para. 16 – 17: ______________________________

II. Analyzing the Paragraphs

◇ *Summarize the information.*

◇ *Generalize the main idea.*

◇ *Find out the topic sentence.*

1. What is the main idea of Paragraph 1?

____

2. What is the main idea of Paragraph 2?

____

3. What is the main idea of Paragraph 3?

____

4. What is the main idea of Paragraph 4, 5 and 6?

____

5. What is the main idea of Paragraph 7, 8 and 9?

____

6. What is the main idea of Paragraph 10 and 11?

____

7. What is the main idea of Paragraph 12 and 13?

____

8. What is the main idea of Paragraph 14 and 15?

____

9. What is the main idea of Paragraph 16 and 17?

____

III. Learning the Language

◇ *Be aware of and sensitive to language variations and varieties.*

◇ *Choose the language as being used in the passage.*

◇ *Learn the best language.*

1. This discovery has been made in the word laboratories of the world. ________ theoretical English professors, but by practical, hard-headed scholars who have been searching for the secrets of success. (Para. 1)

   A) Not by　　B) Not from　　C) By no　　D) By not

2. That one of the easiest and quickest ways to get ahead is by consciously ________ your knowledge of words. (Para. 2)

   A) building up　　B) building　　C) setting up　　D) setting

3. And that from then on it is necessary to have an intelligent plan if progress is to be made. No haphazard hit-or-miss method will ________. (Para. 2)

   A) make it　　B) do

   C) make do with it　　D) do it

4. It has long since been satisfactorily established ________ a high executive does not have a large vocabulary merely because of the opportunities of his position. (Para. 3)

   A) that　　B) it　　C) the one　　D) which

5. That would be putting the cart before the horse. Quite the ________ is true. (Para. 3)

   A) converse　　B) inverse　　C) reverse　　D) diverse

6. The ________ of your vocabulary indicates the degree of your intelligence. (Para. 7)
   A) scope　B) extent　C) range　D) level
7. A pianist may have the most beautiful tunes in his head, but if he had only five keys on his piano he would never get more than a ________ of these tunes out. (Para. 11)
   A) fragment　B) fraction　C) fragrant　D) flagrant
8. And the more words you have ________, the deeper, clearer and more accurate will be your thinking. (Para. 11)
   A) for your command　B) with your command
   C) at your command　D) in your command
9. Words can also change the direction of your life. They have often ________ a man from mediocrity to success. (Para. 15)
   A) risen　B) advanced　C) raised　D) promoted
10. The new and higher position you have won will, in turn, give you a better opportunity ________ your vocabulary. (Para. 16)
   A) to further　B) for furthering
   C) to further enriching　D) for further enriching

IV. Thinking Openly

◇ *Keep your mind open to new ideas.*

◇ *Be receptive to other's opinions.*

◇ *Challenge your own judgment.*

1. If your vocabulary is limited your chances of success are limited. What do you think? (Para. 2)

____

____

2. That the vocabulary of the average person almost stops growing by the middle twenties. Is it true to you? (Para. 2)

____

____

3. Your brain power will increase as you learn to know more words. Do you agree? (Para. 7)

____

____

4. Words are your tools of thought. What do you think? Can you illustrate this? (Para. 10)

____

____

5. And the more words you have at your command, the deeper, clearer and more accurate will be your thinking. What do you think? (Para. 11)

____

____

6. Your words are your personality. Your vocabulary is you. Do you agree? (Para. 12)

____

____

V. Thinking Critically

◇ *Be critical in your thinking.*

◇ *Be skeptical in your thinking.*

◇ *Be introspective in your thinking.*

1. Since the middle twenties, it is necessary to have an intelligent plan if progress in expanding vocabulary is to be made. What is your way of extending your English vocabulary?

____

2. A simple word can destroy a friendship. And words can make an enemy. Do you have such stories to tell?

____

____

3. Words can change one's direction of life. Whose words have the most

fundamental effect on you in your life so far? What is the story?

____

____

4. You may not need eloquence to succeed, but eloquence can surely be of great help to your success. What do you think?

____

____

5. The point(s) that I do not agree with the writer.

____

____

VI. Thinking Independently

◇ *Develop and form ideas or opinions of your own.*

◇ *Be both inductive and deductive in your thinking.*

◇ *Communicate and share with others.*

◇ *Write and present your composition on one of the following topics.*

1. The importance of language ability
2. The words I will never forget
3. The words I will never say again
4. My way of learning English vocabulary
5. One thing I have learned from this passage

Passage 3

KNOWLEDGE AND WISDOM

1 Most people would agree that, although our age far surpasses all previous ages in knowledge, there has been no correlative increase in wisdom. But agreement ceases as soon as we attempt to define "wisdom" and consider means of promoting it.

2 There are several factors that contribute to wisdom. Of these I should put first a sense of proportion: the capacity to take account of all the important factors in a problem and to attach to each its due weight. This has become more difficult than it used to be owing to the extent and complexity of the specialized knowledge required of various kinds of technicians. Suppose you study the composition of the atom from a disinterested desire for knowledge, and incidentally place in the hands of powerful and irresponsible persons the means of destroying the human race. In such ways the pursuit of knowledge may become harmful unless it is combined with wisdom; and wisdom in the sense of comprehensive vision is not necessarily present in specialists in the pursuit of knowledge.

3 Comprehensiveness alone, however, is not enough to constitute wisdom. There must be, also, a certain awareness of the ends of human life. This may be illustrated by the study of history. Many eminent historians have done more harm than good because they viewed facts

through the distorting medium of their own passions. Perhaps one could stretch the comprehensiveness that constitutes wisdom to include not only intellect but also feeling. It is by no means uncommon to find men whose knowledge is wide but whose feelings are narrow. Such men lack what I am calling wisdom.

4 It is not only in public ways, but in private life equally, that wisdom is needed. It is needed in the choice of ends to be pursued and in emancipation from personal prejudice. Even an end which it would be noble to pursue may be pursued unwisely.

5 I think the essence of wisdom is emancipation, as far as possible, from the improper use of our power. We cannot help the egoism of our senses. Sight and sound and touch are bound up with our own bodies and cannot be made impersonal. Our emotions start similarly from ourselves. An infant feels hunger or discomfort and is unaffected except by his own physical condition. Gradually with the years, his horizon widens, and as his thoughts and feelings become less personal and less concerned with his own physical states, he achieves growing wisdom. This is of course a matter of degree. No one can view the world with complete fairness. But it is possible to make a continued approach towards fairness. It is this approach towards fairness that continues growth in wisdom.

6 Can wisdom in this sense be taught? And, if it can, should the teaching of it be one of the aims of education? I should answer both these questions in the affirmative. It might be objected that it is right to hate those who do harm. But if you hate them, it is only too likely that you will become equally harmful; and it is very unlikely that you will induce them to abandon their evil ways. The way-out is through understanding, not through hate. I am not advocating non-resistance. But I am saying that resistance, if it is to be effective in preventing the spread of evil, should be combined with the greatest degree of understanding and the smallest degree of force. Abraham Lincoln conducted a great war without ever departing from what I have been calling wisdom.

7 It is true that the kind of specialized knowledge which is required for various kinds of skill has very little to do with wisdom. With every increase of knowledge and skill, wisdom becomes more necessary, for every such increase expands our capacity of realizing our purposes, and therefore expands our capacity for evil, if our purposes are unwise. The world needs wisdom as it has never needed it before, and if knowledge continues to increase, the world will need wisdom in the future even more than it does now.

(Adapted from *Modern English Reader*)

WORDS AND PHRASES

affirmative *n.*	positive assertion
composition *n.*	constituent; make-up
correlative【kəˈrelətiv】*adj.*	naturally related
distort *v.*	give inaccurate report
emancipation *n.*	act of freeing
incidentally *adv.*	by the way
induce *v.*	persuade somebody to do sth.

I. Understanding the Text

◇ *Understand the subject matter.*

◇ *Read for the main information.*

◇ *Learn the writing technique.*

◇ *Reach the conclusion.*

1. What is the theme of the passage?

____

2. What are the main points made in this passage?

Para. 2 – 3: ______________________________

Para. 4: ______________________________

Para. 5: ______________________________

Para. 6: ______________________________

3. What is the conclusion drawn in this passage?

   Para. 7: ____________________

II. Analyzing the Paragraphs

◇ *Summarize the information.*

◇ *Generalize the main idea.*

◇ *Find out the topic sentence.*

1. What is the main idea of Paragraph 2?

   ____

2. What is the main idea of Paragraph 3?

   ____

3. What is the main idea of Paragraph 4?

   ____

4. What is the main idea of Paragraph 5?

   ____

5. What is the main idea of Paragraph 6?

   ____

6. What is the conclusion drawn in Paragraph 7?

   ____

III. Learning the Language

◇ *Be aware of and sensitive to language variations and varieties.*

◇ *Choose the language as being used in the passage.*

◇ *Learn the best language.*

1. Of these I should put first a sense of proportion: the capacity to ________ account of all the important factors in a problem and to attach to each its due weight. (Para. 2)

   A) get　　B) give　　C) make　　D) take

2. This has become more difficult than it used to be owing to the extent and complexity of the specialized knowledge required ________ various

kinds of technicians. (Para. 2)

A) in B) by C) of D) from

3. In such ways the pursuit of knowledge may become harmful unless it is combined with wisdom; and wisdom in the sense of comprehensive vision is not necessarily ________ in specialists in the pursuit of knowledge. (Para. 2)

A) at present B) present C) presented D) presenting

4. It is by no means uncommon to find men whose knowledge is wide but whose feelings are ________. Such men lack what I am calling wisdom. (Para. 3)

A) narrow B) negative C) positive D) low

5. Gradually with the years, his horizon ________, and as his thoughts and feelings become less personal and less concerned with his own physical states, he achieves growing wisdom. (Para. 5)

A) opens B) widens C) develops D) grows

6. Can wisdom in this sense be taught? And, if it can, should the teaching of it be one of the aims of education? I should answer both these questions ________ the affirmative. (Para. 6)

A) for B) at C) in D) on

7. But if you hate them, it is only too likely that you will become equally harmful; and it is very unlikely that you will ________ them to abandon their evil ways. (Para. 6)

A) introduce B) produce C) deduce D) induce

8. With every increase of knowledge and skill, wisdom becomes more necessary, for every such increase expands our capacity of ________ our purposes, and therefore expands our capacity for evil, if our purposes are unwise. (Para. 7)

A) realizing B) meeting C) making D) satisfying

IV. Thinking Openly

◇ *Keep your mind open to new ideas.*

◇ *Be receptive to other's opinions.*

◇ *Challenge your own judgment.*

1. How do you define wisdom?

____

____

2. What are the means of promoting wisdom?

____

____

3. How does knowledge contribute to wisdom?

____

____

4. It is by no means uncommon to find men whose knowledge is wide but whose feelings are narrow. Such men lack what I am calling wisdom. Who is such a person in your mind? (Para. 3)

____

____

5. In what way is wisdom needed in private life? (Para. 4)

____

____

6. Should the teaching of it (wisdom) be one of the aims of education? What is your viewpoint? (Para. 6)

____

____

V. Thinking Critically

◇ *Be critical in your thinking.*

◇ *Be skeptical in your thinking.*

◇ *Be introspective in your thinking.*

1. Do you agree that the capacity to take account of all the important

factors in a problem and to attach to each its due weight is a factor that contributes to wisdom?

____

____

2. The pursuit of knowledge may become harmful unless it is combined with wisdom; and wisdom in the sense of comprehensive vision is not necessarily present in specialists in the pursuit of knowledge. What do you think?

____

____

3. Comprehensiveness alone, however, is not enough to constitute wisdom. It must also be combined with intellect and feeling. What do you think?

____

____

4. Even an end which it would be noble to pursue may be pursued unwisely. What's your comment on this statement?

____

____

5. But it is possible to make a continued approach towards fairness. It is this approach towards fairness that continues growth in wisdom. What is your opinion?

____

____

6. But if you hate them, it is only too likely that you will become equally harmful; and it is very unlikely that you will induce them to abandon their evil ways. Do you think the same way?

____

____

7. The world needs wisdom as it has never needed it before, and if knowledge continues to increase, the world will need wisdom in the

future even more than it does now. Do you agree with this conclusion?

____

____

VI. Thinking Independently

◇ *Develop and form ideas or opinions of your own.*

◇ *Be both inductive and deductive in your thinking.*

◇ *Communicate and share with others.*

◇ *Write and present your composition on one of the following topics.*

1. On wisdom
2. Wisdom means to get wise
3. Knowledge—the basis of wisdom
4. Wisdom—the aim of knowledge
5. One thing I have learned from this passage

Passage 4

INDIVIDUALS AND MASSES

1 A man or woman makes direct contact with society in two ways: as a member of some familial, professional or religious group, or as a member of a crowd. Groups are capable of being as moral and intelligent as the individuals who form them; a crowd is chaotic, has no purpose of its own and is capable of anything except intelligent action and realistic thinking. Assembled in a crowd, people lose their powers of reasoning and their capacity for moral choice. Their suggestibility is increased to the point where they cease to have any judgment or will of their own. They become very excitable, they lose all sense of individual or collective responsibility, and they are subject to sudden excesses of rage, enthusiasm and panic. In a word, a man in a crowd behaves as though he had swallowed a large dose of some powerful intoxicant. He is a victim of what I have called 'herd-poisoning'. Like alcohol, herd-poison is an active, extravagant drug. The crowd-intoxicated individual escapes from responsibility, intelligence and morality into a kind of frantic, animal mindlessness.

2 Reading is a private, not a collective activity. The writer speaks only to individuals, sitting by themselves in a state of normal sobriety. The orator speaks to masses of individuals, already well-primed with herd-poison. They are at his mercy and, if he knows his business, he can do

what he likes with them.

3 Unlike the masses, intellectuals have a taste for rationality and an interest in facts. Their critical habit of mind makes them resistant to the kind of propaganda that works so well on the majority. Intellectuals are the kind of people who demand evidence and are shocked by logical inconsistencies and fallacies. They regard over-simplification as the original sin of the mind and have no use for the slogans, the unqualified assertions and sweeping generalizations which are the propagandist's stock-in-trade.

4 Philosophy teaches us to feel uncertain about the things that seem to us self-evident. Propaganda, on the other hand, teaches us to accept as self-evident matters about which it would be reasonable to suspend our judgment or to feel doubt. The propagandist must therefore be consistently dogmatic. All his statements are made without qualification. There are no greys in his picture of the world; everything is either diabolically black or celestially white. He must never admit that he might be wrong or that people with a different point of view might be even partially right. Opponents should not be argued with; they should be attacked, shouted down, or if they become too much of a nuisance, liquidated.

5 Virtue and intelligence belong to human beings as individuals freely associating with other individuals in small groups. So do sin and stupidity. But the subhuman mindlessness to which the demagogue makes his appeal, the moral imbecility on which he relies when he goads his victims into action, are characteristic not of men and women as individuals, but of men and women in masses. Mindlessness and moral idiocy are not characteristically human attributes; they are symptoms of herd-poisoning. In all the world's higher religions, salvation and enlightenment are for individuals. The kingdom of heaven is within the mind of a person, not within the collective mindlessness of a crowd.

6 In an age of accelerating over-population, of accelerating over-organization and ever more efficient means of mass communication, how can we

preserve the integrity and reassert the value of the human individual? This is a question that can still be asked and perhaps effectively answered. A generation from now it may be too late to find an answer and perhaps impossible, in the stifling collective climate of that future time, even to ask the question.

(By *Aldus Huxley*)

WORDS AND PHRASES

assertion【əˈsəʃən】*n.*	definite statement
attribute【ˈætribju:t】*n.*	quality; characteristic
celestially【siˈlestjəli】*adv.*	as in heaven
demagogue【ˈdeməgɔg】*n.*	person influencing the common people by making speeches
diabolically【daiəˈbɔlikəli】*adv.*	like a devil
enlightenment【inˈlaitənmənt】*n.*	a true understanding of things
familial【fəˈmiljəl】*adj.*	relating to the family
frantic【ˈfræntik】*adj.*	wildly excited
goad【goud】*v.*	stir up; incite
imbecility【imbəˈsiliti】*n.*	great stupidity
intoxicant【inˈtɔksikənt】*n.*	something which makes one lose control of oneself
liquidate【ˈlikwideit】*v.*	get rid of; kill
sobriety【souˈbraiəti】*n.*	ability to judge things calmly
stifling【ˈstaifliŋ】*adj.*	oppressive; allowing no room for free thought or action
well-primed *adj.*	filled; prepared

I. Understanding the Text

◇ *Understand the subject matter.*

◇ *Read for the main information.*

◇ *Learn the writing technique.*

◇ *Reach the conclusion.*

1. What is the theme of the passage?

____

2. What does the writer intend to say to the reader about individuals and masses?

____

3. What writing technique is used to write this passage?

____

4. What contrasts are made throughout the passage to illustrate the differences between individuals and masses?

   Para. 1: ____

   Para. 2: ____

   Para. 3 –4: ____

   Para. 5: ____

5. What is the conclusion drawn in the passage?

   Para. 6: ____

II. Analyzing the Paragraphs

◇ *Summarize the information.*

◇ *Generalize the main idea.*

◇ *Find out the topic sentence.*

1. What characterize groups and crowds? (Para. 1)

   Groups: ____

   ____

   Crowds: ____

   ____

2. What is the difference between a writer and an orator? (Para. 2)

   Writer: ____

   ____

   Orator: ____

   ____

3. How are intellectuals different from propagandists? (Para. 3 – 4)

Intellectuals: ____

____

Propagandists: ____

____

4. How do individuals differ from masses? (Para. 5)

Individuals: ____

____

Masses: ____

____

5. What are the factors that make it difficult to preserve the integrity and reassert the value of the human individual? (Para. 6)

____

____

III. Learning the Language

◇ *Be aware of and sensitive to language variations and varieties.*

◇ *Choose the language as being used in the passage.*

◇ *Learn the best language.*

1. ________ in a crowd, people lose their powers of reasoning and their capacity for moral choice. (Para. 1)

   A) Assembling　　B) To assemble

   C) Assembled　　D) To be assembled

2. They become very excitable, they lose all sense of individual or collective responsibility, they ________ sudden excesses of rage, enthusiasm and panic. (Para. 1)

   A) are likely to　　B) are liable to　　C) are subject to　　D) are apt to

3. Reading is a private, not a collective activity. The writer speaks only to individuals, ________ themselves in a state of normal sobriety. (Para. 2)

   A) to sit by　　B) by sitting　　C) who sit by　　D) sitting by

4. The orator speaks to masses of individuals, already well-primed with

herd-poison. They are ________ and, if he knows his business, he can do what he likes with them. (Para. 2)

A) in his mercy B) for his mercy
C) to his mercy D) at his mercy

5. Unlike the masses, intellectuals ________ rationality and an interest in facts. (Para. 3)

A) have a taste in B) have a taste of
C) have a taste with D) have a taste for

6. They regard over-simplification as the original sin of the mind and have no use for the slogans, the unqualified assertions and sweeping generalizations which are the propagandist's ________. (Para. 3)

A) stock and trade B) stock for trade
C) stock of trade D) stock-in-trade

7. There are no greys in his picture of the world; everything is either diabolically black or ________ white. (Para. 4)

A) celestially B) terrestrially
C) elastically D) theoretically

8. Virtue and intelligence belong to human beings as individuals freely associating with other individuals in small groups. So ________ sin and stupidity. (Para. 5)

A) do B) are C) does D) is

9. But the subhuman mindlessness to which the demagogue makes his appeal, the moral imbecility on which he relies when he goads his victim into action, ________ men and women as individuals, but of men and women in masses. (Para. 5)

A) are characteristic not of B) are not characteristic of
C) are characteristic not with D) are not characteristic with

10. Mindlessness and moral idiocy are not characteristically human ________; they are symptoms of herd-poisoning. (Para. 5)

A) attribute B) attributes
C) attributions D) attribution

IV. Thinking Openly

◇ *Keep your mind open to new ideas.*

◇ *Be receptive to other's opinions.*

◇ *Challenge your own judgment.*

1. People in a crowd are subject to sudden excesses of rage, enthusiasm and panic. What do you think? (Para. 1)

____

____

2. Reading is a private, not a collective activity. In what way is reading a private activity? (Para. 2)

____

____

3. Unlike the masses, intellectuals have a taste for rationality and an interest in facts. What's your comment? (Para. 3)

____

____

4. To a propagandist, there are no grays in his picture of the world; everything is either diabolically black or celestially white. What do you think? (Para. 4)

____

____

V. Thinking Critically

◇ *Be critical in your thinking.*

◇ *Be skeptical in your thinking.*

◇ *Be introspective in your thinking.*

1. Do you think of yourself more as an individual in groups or one in masses?

____

____

2. Which of the following fallacies are you more likely to commit: logical inconsistencies, over-simplification, unqualified assertions, and sweeping generalizations?

____

____

3. In an age of accelerating over-population, of accelerating over-organization and ever more efficient means of mass communication, it is more difficult to preserve the integrity and reassert the value of the human individual. Why?

____

____

4. The point(s) that I do not agree with the writer.

____

____

VI. Thinking Independently

◇ *Develop and form ideas or opinions of your own.*

◇ *Be both inductive and deductive in your thinking.*

◇ *Communicate and share with others.*

◇ *Write and present your composition on one of the following topics.*

1. One who travels alone travels farthest
2. Being in a group gives me a sense of belonging
3. Individual responsibility or collective responsibility
4. Being alone doesn't mean being lonely
5. One thing I have learned from the passage

Passage 5

GROWING UP IS HARD TO DO

1 I'd like to think I'll be a better father, that I have learned from my Dad's mistakes. On most days I can buy that. But there are times when I look in the mirror and see who I've become, and think of who he's always been, and I'm not so sure. You can't pick up a newspaper without reading of the nightmare that is child abuse, or how alcohol is ripping families apart. I see these articles and feel a little foolish for my anger. My father was neither abusive nor alcoholic. He was simply absent.

2 Dad did always love me. He still does—or so he says on the rare occasions when we catch one another on the phone. He had his priorities when I was young, and now I have mine. I'm in jail, and my primary concern is my trial. I'm sure he understands. I always did.

3 My parent married when they were young and idealistic. I was only 2 when they gave up on their marriage and went their separate ways. I stayed with Mom. Dad probably wanted it that way, as he needed to "stretch his wings" (his words, not mine).

4 I don't remember much of him in the early days except that he was my hero. I do recall the stories I used to tell the other kids about an important and powerful man. He used to fly in on a moment's notice. I'd see him for a few precious hours. He drove flashy rental cars, wore

expensive suits and took me to top-dollar restaurants. It enthralled me. This man was so big, so much larger than life. He was my dad and, in my eyes, the king of the world. I recently asked Mom how many monthly child-support payments he made in those years of absence. Her face drew into a tight smile, the kind that only painful memories can bring. She said she wasn't sure, but she could probably count the number on one hand. I guess he had other things to spend money on.

5 As I grew older, the visits became more and more infrequent, sometimes a year apart. Nonetheless, what they lacked in quantity, Dad made up for in quality—or some cruel parody of it. He flew in from Los Angeles, New York or San Francisco. He dropped names left and right, always on the brink of really big success. He remained my hero.

6 Such is the innocence of youth that when he called, always a few weeks after Christmas or my birthday, and told me the package I never received "must have gotten lost in the mail," I believed him wholeheartedly. Until I was 13 or 14 years old, I was afraid to mail a letter for fear the same fate would befall it. But as the years rolled on, the truth about the letters and packages, the truth about everything, became painfully obvious. I tried for a while to stick my head in the sand. This wasn't the same as learning about Santa Claus or the Easter Bunny.

7 The road from realization to acceptance is a lot longer than it looks. I've been on it for the past five years, and I'm not all that far from where I started. "The past is the past" is a nice catch phrase, and one I've tried in vain to make myself believe. "Saying and doing are two different things" is another winner, but it's easier to digest. My father and I have a hard journey ahead of us, provided we can find the time. There is sorrow in his voice when we discuss the past and I know that if he had it to do over, he'd do his best to do it right. Second chances are few, and it's much easier to do it right the first time. That's become painfully obvious to me as I live with the consequences of my own mistakes every day.

8 My dad loved me as only a father can love a son. I don't question that. But he was also a self-centered, egocentric s. o. b. who let me down when I needed him most. A part of me will always be that kid at the window waiting and waiting with his nose pressed against the glass. Knowing that if Dad said he was coming, he was coming; but waking up curled beneath the window, alone.

9 I don't want to sit and cry about the scars his actions may have left. I'd like to believe the only real damage done was to our relationship. But I have a very hard time letting people in. Trust is not an easy word for me to say, and it's almost impossible for me to feel it. I learned a hard lesson a long time ago. It's not one I'll risk learning again.

10 Now that I'm older, ironically, the tables have turned. It's Dad who seeks out his son, and it's he who is let down. Not so long ago, we took a trip, my dad and I. I was in trouble with the law, and Dad flew in from New York to help me. We drove from my grandparents' home in North Carolina to my mother's house in Atlanta. It was a gallant gesture, but neither of us could find our way around the wall that we'd built. We talked of business things, politics, a weakening dollar, you know, the important things. Eventually the conversation turned to the past, and at one point this baldish but still distinguished 43-year-old man looked at his 19-year-old son, who outweighs him by 30 pounds, and asked with tears in his eyes, "How did you grow up so fast? What happened to my little boy?" I suppose I could have said something witty about absence or painful about time. But looked at this man who was once my hero, and I saw the gray in what's left of his hair and the wrinkles around his eyes. I understood his frustration at being unable to solve my problems. It was then I began to replace anger with compassion as I realized he was just as human, as vulnerable, as I.

11 I love my father, but looking in the mirror sometimes I get a little scared. We are just so damned with much alike. Father's Day is right around the corner. There are a lot of kids thinking about their heroes, and

I hope a lot of heroes are thinking about their kids. Divorce is a painful fact of life and all too common. Probably there are many kids who don't see much of dad, and a fair amount of dads who don't visit as they should. If I'm lucky, a handful of those fathers are reading this. Your kids will love you whether you make it or not; that is the nature of being a hero. But maybe you should take time to consider how important whatever else you've got planned is. We do grow up fast. Just ask my dad, or better yet, ask yours.

WORDS AND PHRASES

befall【biˈfɔːl】*v.*	happen
brink【briŋk】*n.*	verge; edge
catch phrase	a phrase that catches attention
compassion【kəmˈpæʃən】*n.*	pity; sympathy
Easter Bunny	复活节的小兔子(礼物)
egocentric【ˌigəusɛntrik】*adj.*	viewing everything in relation to oneself
enthrall【inˈθrɔːl】*v.*	captivate
flashy【ˈflæʃi】*adj.*	giving a momentary or superficial impression
gallant【ˈgælənt】*adj.*	brave; noble
parody【ˈpærədi】*n.*	a humorous imitation
s. o. b. (Am sl.)	son of a bitch
stick one's head in the sand	pay little or no attention
vulnerable【ˈvʌlnərəbl】*adj.*	that can be wounded or injured

I. Understanding the Text

◇ *Understand the subject matter.*

◇ *Read for the main information.*

◇ *Learn the writing technique.*

◇ *Reach the conclusion.*

1. What is the type of writing of this passage?

____

2. What are the four typts/genres of writing?

____

3. What is the CONTEXT of this narration?

____

4. What is the SELECTION OF DETAILS of this narration?

   Para. 4: ______________________________________

   Para. 8: ______________________________________

   Para. 10: _____________________________________

5. What is the POINT OF VIEW of this narration?

____

6. What is the PURPOSE of this narration?

____

7. What does the title of this narration intend to say?

____

II. Analyzing the Paragraphs

◇ *Summarize the information.*

◇ *Generalize the main idea.*

◇ *Find out the topic sentence.*

1. What does the writer intend to introduce? (Para. 1)

____

2. What is the main idea of Para. 2?

____

3. What is the main idea of Para. 3?

____

4. What is the main idea of Para. 4?

____

5. What is the main idea of Para. 5?

____

6. What happened between father and son? (Para. 6)

____

7. What is Para. 7 all about?

____

8. What has been narrated in Para. 8?

____

9. What is the hard lesson the child had learned? (Para. 9)

____

10. What finally happened to the father-son relationship? (Para. 10)

____

III. Learning the Language

◇ *Be aware of and sensitive to language variations and varieties.*

◇ *Choose the language as being used in the passage.*

◇ *Learn the best language.*

1. You can't pick up a newspaper without reading of the nightmare that is child abuse, or how alcohol is ________ families apart. (Para. 1)

   A) ripping　　B) splitting　　C) breaking　　D) cracking

2. My parent married when they were young and idealistic. I was only 2 when they gave up on their marriage and went their ________ ways. (Para. 3)

   A) separate　　B) own　　C) different　　D) two

3. He used to fly in ________. (Para. 4)

   A) in a moment's notice　　B) with a moment's notice

   C) on a moment's notice　　D) for a moment's notice

4. Her face ________ a tight smile, the kind that only painful memories can bring. (Para. 4)

   A) turned into　　B) drew into　　C) changed into　　D) shifted into

5. He dropped names left and right, always ________ of really big success. He remained my hero. (Para. 5)

   A) on the edge　　B) on the verge　　C) on the brink　　D) on the stage

6. ________ is the innocence of youth that when he called, always a few

weeks after Christmas or my birthday, and told me the package I never received "must have gotten lost in the mail," I believed him wholeheartedly. (Para. 6)

A) As B) Thus C) Such D) So

7. Until I was 13 or 14 years old, I was afraid to mail a letter for fear the same fate would ________ it. (Para. 6)

A) occur B) happen C) fall D) befall

8. But as the years ________, the truth about the letters and packages, the truth about everything, became painfully obvious. (Para. 6)

A) went on B) rolled on C) passed on D) flew on

9. Now that I'm older, ironically, the tables have ________. It's Dad who seeks out his son. (Para. 10)

A) turned B) been turned

C) changed D) been changed

10. Father's Day is ________ around the corner. There are a lot of kids thinking about their heroes, and I hope a lot of heroes are thinking about their kids. (Para. 11)

A) right B) just C) but D) again

IV. Thinking Openly

◇ *Keep your mind open to new ideas.*

◇ *Be receptive to other's opinions.*

◇ *Challenge your own judgment.*

1. My parent married when they were young and idealistic. What have you learned from this sentence? (Para. 3)

____

____

2. I don't remember much of him in the early days except that he(the father) was my hero. What is the most distinctive part of your father? (Para. 4)

____

____

3. The road from realization to acceptance is a lot longer than it looks. What does this sentence refer to? Do you have a similar experience? (Para. 7)

____

____

4. "The past is the past" is a nice catch phrase, and one I've tried in vain to make myself believe. Do you have an it's-easier-to-say-than-done story to tell? (Para. 7)

____

____

5. Second chances are few, and it's much easier to do it right the first time. What's your understanding of this sentence? (Para. 7)

____

____

V. Thinking Critically

◇ *Be critical in your thinking.*

◇ *Be skeptical in your thinking.*

◇ *Be introspective in your thinking.*

1. I'd like to think I'll be a better father, that I have learned from my Dad's mistakes. Are you sure that you can be a better father or mother?

____

____

2. Have you ever looked at yourself in the mirror and see whom you've become? What have you found out?

____

____

3. Do you have an unforgettable childhood memory to share with us? What is it?

____

____

4. Trust is not an easy word for me to say, and it's almost impossible for me to feel it. What's your comment?

____

____

5. Do you happen to have a self-centered person around you? How do you try to manage the personal relationship with him/her?

____

____

VI. Thinking Independently

◇ *Develop and form ideas or opinions of your own.*

◇ *Be both inductive and deductive in your thinking.*

◇ *Communicate and share with others.*

◇ *Write and present your composition on one of the following topics.*

1. Saying and doing are two different things
2. An unforgettable childhood memory
3. Divorce is a painful experience of life
4. Things we have to do right the first time
5. Learn to forgive makes us more human
6. Love and hatred are just one step aside
7. One thing I have learned from this passage

Passage 6

LIES AND TRUTH

1 What is truth? — and the opposite question that goes with it: what makes a lie? Philosophers, teachers, and religious leaders from all cultures and all periods of history have offered many answers to these questions. Among Euro-North-American writers, there is a general agreement on two points. The first is that what we call "a lie" must have been told intentionally—that is, if someone tells an untruth but they believe it to be true, we don't consider them a liar. The second point is that practically everyone lies, and lies frequently. But there the agreement ends.

2 One rather extreme point of view is that lying is always bad and that we should try to find ways to avoid doing it. The reason is that lying hurts not only the listener, but also the liar. Each lie makes the next one easier to tell, and the liar comes not only to disrespect herself, but to mistrust others, whom she believes will lie as easily as she. In a society where lying is common, trust becomes impossible, and without trust, cooperation cannot exist. Furthermore, by lying to people, we remove their power to make important choices about how to spend money, what future career to take, what medical treatment to choose.

3 Toward the opposite extreme is the position that although some lies are evil, many others are not—in fact, they are necessary to hold our society

together. We lie in harmless ways to protect each other's feelings and to better our relationships. These are not lies that try to hurt others. We laugh at the boss's joke which we have heard before and which she doesn't tell very well; we pretend interest in a friend's story of something uninteresting that happened to him. If someone asks us a question that is very personal and is none of their business, we may lie in response. Sometimes we lie to protect the reputation or even the life of another person. On a larger scale, government may protect national security by lying.

4 Each person seems to have some point at which they draw the line between an acceptable lie and a bad lie. Obviously, this point varies from individual to individual and from culture to culture. A sometimes painful part of growing up is realizing that not everyone shares your own individual definition of honesty. Your parents and your culture may teach you that liars will suffer, but as you go through life, you find that often they don't: in fact, dishonest people often seem to prosper more than honest ones. What are you to do with this realization? It may make your moral beliefs look weak and silly in comparison, and you may begin to question them. It takes a great deal of strength and courage to continue living an honest life in the face of such a reality.

5 There are many ways to categorize lies, but here is a fairly simple one.

6 Little white lies: This is our name for lies that we consider harmless and socially acceptable. They are usually told to protect the liar or the feelings of the listener. Most of them would be considered social lies, and they include apologies and excuses: "I tried to call you, but your line was busy." "You're kidding! You don't look like you've gained a pound." Some people, however, would consider it acceptable to lie to save themselves from responsibility in a business transaction: "After I got it home, I noticed that it was broken, so I'm returning it and would like my money back."

7 Occasionally a "little white lie" may have a very profound effect on

the lives of the listeners, and may even backfire. Author Stephanie Ericsson tells of the well-meaning U. S. Army sergeant who told a lie about one of his men who had been killed in action. The sergeant reported the man as "missing in action," not killed, so that the military would continue sending money to the dead man's family every month. What he didn't consider was that because of his lie, the family continued to live in that narrow space between hope and loss, always watching for the mail or jumping when the telephone or the doorbell rang. They never were able to go through the normal process of sorrowing for, and then accepting, the death of their father and husband. The wife never remarried. Which was worse, the lie or the truth? Did the sergeant have the right to do what he did to them?

8 What we really mean when we call an untruth a "little white lie" is that we think it was justifiable. Into this category fall many of the lies told within the walls of government. A person may lie to government, or a government official may lie to the public, and believe that by doing so, he becomes a hero. Clearly, however, one person's "little white lie" is another person's "dirty lie." That brings us to the second category.

9 Dirty lies: These are lies told with intent to harm the listener or a third party and to benefit the liar. Into this category fall the lies of some dishonest salespersons, mechanics, repairmen; husbands or wives who are having an affair with someone else; teenagers who lie to get out of the house in order to do things that their parents would die if they knew about; drug addicts who beg family members for money to support their habit. Dirty lies may be told to improve one person's reputation by destroying another's, to hurt a colleague's chances of promotion so that the liar will be advanced.

10 Lies of omission: Some people believe that lying covers not only what you say, but also what you choose not to say. If you're trying to sell a car that burns a lot of oil, but the buyers don't ask about that particular feature, is it a lie not to tell them? In the United States, a favorite place

to withhold the truth is on people's income tax returns. The government considers this an unquestionable lie and if caught, these people are severely punished. If omission can be lying, history books are great liars. Until recently, most U. S. history textbooks painted Christopher Columbus purely as a hero, the man who "discovered America," and had nothing to say about his darker side.

11 False promises: This category is made up of promises that the promiser knows are false, that he has no intention of keeping even as the words leave his lips. While some are fairly harmless and social, others are taken seriously and can hurt the listener: "I'll never do it again, I promise." Advertisers and politicians suffer from terrible stereotypes because of the false promises of some of their number: "Lose 50 pounds in two weeks." "Read my lips: No new taxes." Probably everyone would agree that if we make a promise but have no intention of keeping it, we lie. But what if we really do plan to keep it, and then something happens to prevent it? Consider the journalist who promises not to identify his sources, but then is pressured by his newspaper or by the law. How far should he go to keep his word? If he breaks his promise, is he dishonest?

12 Lies to oneself: This is perhaps the saddest and most pathetic kind of lying. These are the lies that prevent us from making needed changes in ourselves: "I know I drank/spent/ate too much yesterday, but I can control it any time I really want to." But there is a fine line between normal dreams and ambitions on the one hand, and deceiving ourselves on the other, and we have to be careful where we draw it. It's common for young people to dream of rising to the top of their company, of winning a Nobel Prize, of becoming famous or rich; but is that self-deception, or simply human nature? Were they lying to themselves? More likely, they really believed that such a future was open to them, because they had seen it happen to others. We shouldn't be too hard on ourselves, but if we have turned a blind eye to our faults, we should take an honest look in

the mirror.

13 There is no question that the terms "lying" and "honesty" have definitions that vary across cultural boundaries. Members of one culture may stereotype members of another as "great liars," "untrustworthy," or "afraid to face the truth." But what may lie behind these differences is that one culture values factual information even if it hurts, while another places more value on sensitivity to other people's feelings. While the members of each culture believe that of course their values are the right ones, they are unlikely to convince members of other cultures to change over. And that's "the truth."

WORDS AND PHRASES

backfire【ˈbækfaiə】*v.*	have the opposite result
categorize【ˈkætəgəraiz】*v.*	put into groups
justifiable【ˌdʒʌstiˈfaiəbl】*adj.*	be justified
liar【laiə】*n.*	a person who tells a lie
omission【əˈmiʃən】*n.*	something omitted
pathetic【pəˈθetik】*adj.*	causing a feeling of pity or sorrow
profound【prəˈfaund】*adj.*	very deep
sergeant【ˈsaːdʒənt】*n.*	an officer in the army
stereotype【ˈsteriətaip】*n.*	have a fixed pattern
transaction【trænˈzækʃən】*n.*	a deal in business
turn a blind eye (to)	pay no attention to

I. Understanding the Text

◇ *Understand the subject matter.*

◇ *Read for the main information.*

◇ *Learn the writing technique.*

◇ *Reach the conclusion.*

1. What is the theme of this passage?

____

2. What are the main points made in this passage?

Para. 1: ______________________________

Para. 2 – 3: ______________________________

Para. 4: ______________________________

Para. 5 – 12: ______________________________

3. What are the concluding remarks related to lying?

Para. 13: ______________________________

II. Analyzing the Paragraphs

◇ *Summarize the information.*

◇ *Generalize the main idea.*

◇ *Find out the topic sentence.*

1. What is the main idea of Para. 1?

____

2. What is the main idea of Para. 2?

____

3. What is the main idea of Para. 3?

____

4. What is the main idea of Para. 4?

____

5. What is the topic of Para. 6, 7 and 8?

____

6. What is the topic of Para. 9?

____

7. What is the topic of Para. 10?

____

8. What is the topic of Para. 11?

____

9. What is the topic of Para. 12?

____

III. Learning the Language

◇ *Be aware of and sensitive to language variations and varieties.*

◇ *Choose the language as being used in the passage.*

◇ *Learn the best language.*

1. What is truth? — and the opposite question that ________ it: what makes a lie? (Para. 1)

   A) takes with B) comes with C) goes with D) works with

2. One rather extreme point of view is that lying is always bad and that we should try to find ways to avoid ________ it. (Para. 2)

   A) doing B) to do C) making D) to make

3. ________ a larger scale, government may protect national security by lying. (Para. 3)

   A) In B) On C) At D) With

4. Each person seems to have some ________ at which they draw the line between an acceptable lie and a bad lie. (Para. 4)

   A) occasions B) occasion C) points D) point

5. What he didn't consider was that because of his lie, the family continued to live ________ between hope and loss, always watching for the mail or jumping when the telephone or the doorbell rang. (Para. 7)

   A) in that narrow space B) in that narrow place
   C) in that narrow hope D) in that narrow chance

6. Into this category ________ many of the lies told within the walls of government. (Para. 8)

   A) comc B) comes C) fall D) falls

7. Dirty lies may be told to ________ one person's reputation by destroying another's, to hurt a colleague's chances of promotion so that the liar will be advanced. (Para. 9)

   A) change B) mend C) create D) improve

8. But there is a fine line between normal dreams and ambitions on the one hand, and deceiving ourselves on the other, and we have to be

careful where we ________ it. (Para. 12)

A) draw B) make C) produce D) put

9. We shouldn't be too hard on ourselves, but if we have ________ our faults, we should take an honest look in the mirror. (Para. 12)

A) turned a blind eye to B) turned blind eyes to

C) given a blind eye to D) given blind eyes to

10. But what may lie behind these differences is that one culture values factual information even if it hurts, while another ________ more value on sensitivity to other people's feelings. (Para. 13)

A) takes B) places C) lays D) rests

IV. Thinking Openly

◇ *Keep your mind open to new ideas.*

◇ *Be receptive to other's opinions.*

◇ *Challenge your own judgment.*

1. What is the near definition of lying given in Para 1?

____

____

2. Each lie makes the next one easier to tell. Why? (Para. 2)

____

____

3. In a society where lying is common, trust becomes impossible, and without trust, cooperation cannot exist. What do you think of this statement? (Para. 2)

____

____

4. In reality, dishonest people often seem to prosper more than honest ones. What are you to do with this realization? (Para. 4)

____

____

5. Which was worse, the lie or the truth? Did the sergeant have the right

to do what he did to them? (Para. 7)

____

____

6. One person's "little white lie" is another's "dirty lie." What's your comment? (Para. 8)

____

____

7. Lies to oneself: This is perhaps the saddest and most pathetic kind of lying. Why? (Para. 12)

____

____

V. Thinking Critically

◇ *Be critical in your thinking.*

◇ *Be skeptical in your thinking.*

◇ *Be introspective in your thinking.*

1. Practically everyone lies, and lies frequently. Do you lie frequently? What lies do you often tell?

____

____

2. On a larger scale, government may protect national security by lying. Do you think governments are justified to lie?

____

____

3. Do you consider "lies of omission" as lying?

____

____

4. Have you ever made a "false promise"? What is it?

____

____

5. Do you think "lies to oneself" is part of human nature? What are such

lies that you have told to yourself?

6. One culture values factual information even if it hurts, while another places more value on sensitivity to other people's feelings. What do you think of our Chinese culture in this regard?

7. The point(s) that I do not agree with the writer.

VI. Thinking Independently

◇ *Develop and form ideas or opinions of your own.*

◇ *Be both inductive and deductive in your thinking.*

◇ *Communicate and share with others.*

◇ *Write and present your composition on one of the following topics.*

1. My view about lying
2. An occasion on which I prefer to be lied
3. One person's 'little white lie' is another's 'dirty lie'
4. Honesty is my value
5. One lie I will never tell again
6. One thing I have learned from this passage

Passage 7

YOUR KEY TO A BETTER LIFE

1 The most important psychological discovery of this century is the discovery of the "self-image." Whether we realize it or not, each of us carries about with us a mental blueprint or picture of ourselves. It may be vague and ill-defined to our conscious gaze. In fact, it may not be consciously recognizable at all. But it is there, complete down to the last detail. This self-image is our own conception of the "sort of person I am." It has been built up from our own beliefs about ourselves. But most of these beliefs about ourselves have unconsciously been formed from our past experiences, our successes and failures, our humiliations, our triumphs, and the way other people have reacted to us, especially in early childhood. From all these we mentally construct a "self" (or a picture of a self). Once an idea or a belief about ourselves goes into this picture it becomes "true", as far as we personally are concerned. We do not question its validity, but proceed to act upon it just as if it were true.

2 This self-image becomes a golden key to living a better life because of two important discoveries: All your actions, feelings, behavior—even your abilities—are always consistent with this self-image. In short, you will "act like" the sort of person you conceive yourself to be. Not only this, but you literally cannot act otherwise, in spite of all your conscious

efforts or will power. The man who conceives himself to be a "failure type person" will find some way to fail, in spite of all his good intentions, or his will power, even if opportunity is literally dumped in his lap. The person who conceives himself to be a victim of injustice, or one "who was meant to suffer" will invariably find circumstances to verify his opinions.

3 The self-image is a "premise," a base, or a foundation upon which your entire personality, your behavior, and even your circumstances are built. Because of this our experiences seem to verify, and thereby strengthen our self-images, and a vicious or a beneficent cycle, as the case may be, is set up.

4 For example, a schoolboy who sees himself as an "F" type student, or one who is "dumb" in mathematics, will invariably find that his report card bears him out. He then has "proof". A young girl who has an image of herself as the sort of person nobody likes, will find indeed that she is avoided at the school dance. She literally invites rejection. Her woebegone expression, her hang-dog manner, her over-anxiousness to please, or perhaps her unconscious hostility towards those she anticipates will affront her all act to drive away those whom she would attract. In the same manner, a salesman or a businessman will also find that his actual experiences tend to "prove" his self-image is correct.

5 Because of this objective "proof" it very seldom occurs to a person that his trouble lies in his self-image or his own evaluation of himself. Tell the schoolboy that he only "thinks" he cannot master algebra, and he will doubt your sanity. He has tried and tried, and still his report card tells the story. Tell the salesman that it is only an idea that he cannot earn more than a certain figure, and can prove you wrong by his order book. He knows only too well how hard he has tried and failed. Yet, as we shall see later, almost miraculous changes have occurred both in grades of students, and in the earning capacity of salesmen—when they were prevailed upon to change their self-images.

6 The sell-image can be changed. Numerous case histories have shown

that one is never too young nor too old to change his self-image and thereby start to live a new life.

7 One of the reasons it has seemed so difficult for a person to change his habits, his personality, or his way of life, has been that heretofore nearly all efforts at change have been directed to the circumference of the self, so to speak, rather than to the center. Numerous patients have said to me something like the following: If you are talking about 'positive thinking', I've tried that before, and it just doesn't work for me." However, a little questioning invariably brings out that these individuals have employed "positive thinking," or attempted to employ it, either upon particular external circumstances, or upon some particular habit or character defect("I will get that job." I will be more calm and relaxed in the future." "This business venture will turn out right for me," etc.) But they had never thought to change their thinking of the "self" which was to accomplish these things.

8 Jesus warned us about the folly of putting a patch of new material upon an old garment, or of putting new wine into old bottles. "Positive thinking" cannot be used effectively as a patch or a crutch to the same old self-image. In fact, it is literally impossible to really think positively about a particular situation, as long as you hold a negative concept of self. And, numerous experiments have shown that once the concept of self is changed, other things consistent with the new concept of self, are accomplished easily and without strain.

9 One of the earliest and most convincing experiments along this line was conducted by the late Prescott Lecky, one of the pioneers in self-image psychology. Lecky conceived of the personality as a "system of ideas", all of which must seem to be consistent with each other. Ideas which are inconsistent with the system are rejected, not believed, and not acted upon. Ideas which seem to be consistent with the system are accepted. At the very center of this system of ideas—the keystone—the base upon which all else is built, is the individual's "ego ideal", his

"self-image", or his conception of himself. Lecky was a school teacher and had an opportunity to test his theory upon thousands of students.

10 Lecky theorized that if a student had trouble learning a certain subject, it could be because (from the student's point of view) it would be inconsistent for him to learn it. Lecky believed, however, that if you could change the student's self-conception, which underlies this viewpoint, his attitude toward the subject would change accordingly. If the student could be induced to change his self-definition, his learning ability should also change. This proved to be the case. One student who misspelled 55 words out of a hundred and flunked so many subjects that he lost credit for a year, made a general average of 91 the next year and became one of the best spellers in school. A boy who was dropped from one college because of poor grades, entered Columbia and became a straight "A" student. A girl who had flunked Latin four times, after three talks with the school counselor, finished with a grade of 84. A boy who was told by a testing bureau that he had no aptitude for English, won honorable mention the next year for a literary prize.

11 The trouble with these students was not that they were dumb, or lacking in basic aptitudes. The trouble was an inadequate self-image.

WORDS AND PHRASES

a straight "A" student	one who has the highest grade in all courses
affront【əˈfrʌnt】*v.*	insult openly
algebra【ˈældʒibrə】*n.*	代数
bear out	show to be right; confirm
beneficent【biˈnefisənt】*adj.*	doing good
case history	a record of someone suffering from an illness or social difficulties
circumference【səˈkʌmfərəns】*n.*	the boundary line of a circle
conceive of	consider; think of

crutch[krʌtʃ] *n.*	a support to help a lame person to walk
down to the last detail	in every detail
dumb[dʌm] *adj.*	slow in understanding; stupid
dump in sb's lap	make a lucky event come to a person with no effort of his own
hang-dog *adj.*	ashamed; guilty
heretofore[ˌhiətuːˈfɔ] *adv.*	until now
honorable mention	an honorary award next below those that win prizes
humiliation[hjuːˌmiliˈeiʃən] *n.*	disgrace; shame
miraculous *adj.*	extraordinary and marvelous
premise[ˈpremis] *n.*	a statement assumed to be true or used to draw conclusion
prevail upon	persuade
sanity[ˈsænəti] *n.*	the state of having a healthy mind
strain[strein] *n.*	too much effort
verify[ˈverifai] *v.*	prove to be true
woebegone[ˈwəubigɔn] *adj.*	looking sad or sorrowful or wretched

I. Understanding the Text

◇ *Understand the subject matter.*

◇ *Read for the main information.*

◇ *Learn the writing technique.*

◇ *Reach the conclusion.*

1. What is the theme of this passage?

____

2. What are the main points made in this passage?

Para. 1: ______________________________

Para. 2 – 5: ______________________________

Para. 6: ______________________________

Para. 7 – 11: ______________________________

II. Analyzing the Paragraphs

◇ *Summarize the information.*

◇ *Generalize the main idea.*

◇ *Find out the topic sentence.*

1. What is the main idea of Paragraph 1?

____

2. What is the main idea of Paragraph 2?

____

3. What is the main idea of Paragraph 3, 4 and 5?

____

4. What is the main idea of Paragraph 6?

____

5. What is the main idea of Paragraph 7 and 8?

____

6. What is the main idea of Paragraph 9?

____

7. What is the main idea of Paragraph 10 and 11?

____

III. Learning the Language

◇ *Be aware of and sensitive to language variations and varieties.*

◇ *Choose the language as being used in the passage.*

◇ *Learn the best language.*

1. All your actions, feelings, behavior—even your abilities—are always ________ this self-image. (Para. 2)

   A) consistent of　　　　B) consistent to

   C) consistent in　　　　D) consistent with

2. In short, you will "act like" the sort of person you conceive yourself to be. Not only this, but you literally cannot ________, in spite of all your conscious efforts or will power. (Para. 2)

   A) act otherwise　　　　B) behave otherwise

   C) perform otherwise　　D) conduct otherwise

3. The man who conceives himself to be a "failure type person" will find some way to fail, in spite of all his good intentions, or his will power, even if opportunity is literally ________. (Para. 2)

   A) dumped in his leg   B) dumped in his lap
   C) dumped in his legs   D) dumped in his laps

4. The person who conceives himself to be a victim of injustice, or one "who was meant to suffer" will invariably find circumstances to ________ his opinions. (Para. 2)

   A) certify   B) confirm   C) testify   D) verify

5. Because of this our experiences seem to verify, and thereby strengthen our self-image, and a vicious or a ________, as the case may be, is set up. (Para. 3)

   A) beneficiary circle   B) beneficial cycle
   C) beneficent circle   D) beneficent cycle

6. For example, a schoolboy who sees himself as an "F" type student, or one who is "dump" in mathematics, will invariably find that his report card ________. (Para. 4)

   A) tears him out   B) bears him out
   C) tears him off   D) bears him off

7. Yet, as we shall see later, almost miraculous changes have occurred both in grades of students, and in the earning capacity of salesmen—when they were ________ to change their self-images. (Para. 5)

   A) prevailed upon   B) prevailing upon
   C) pervaded upon   D) pervading upon

8. And, numerous experiments have shown that once the concept of self is changed, other things consistent with the new concept of self, are accomplished easily and without ________. (Para. 8)

   A) strain   B) stain   C) restrain   D) detain

9. Lecky ________ the personality as a "system of ideas", all of which must seem to be consistent with each other. (Para. 9)

   A) received of   B) deceived of   C) conceived of   D) perceived of

10. The trouble with these students was ________ they were dumb, or lacking in basic aptitudes. The trouble was an inadequate self-image. (Para. 11)

A) either B) that

C) either that D) not that

IV. Thinking Openly

◇ *Keep your mind open to new ideas.*

◇ *Be receptive to other's opinions.*

◇ *Challenge your own judgment.*

1. All your actions, feelings, behavior—even your abilities—are always consistent with your self-image. What do you think? (Para. 2)

____

____

2. In short, you will "act like" the sort of person you conceive yourself to be. Not only this, but you literally cannot act otherwise. Do you find it true? (Para. 2)

____

____

3. Once our self-image is built up, a vicious or a beneficent cycle is set up. What can you learn from this statement? (Para. 3)

____

____

4. The self-image is a "premise," a base, or a foundation upon which your entire personality, your behavior, and even your circumstances are built. What do you think? (Para. 3)

____

____

5. A young girl who has an image of herself as the sort of person nobody likes, will find indeed that she is avoided at the school dance. She literally invites rejection. Have you ever seen such a person? (Para. 4)

____

____

6. You can hardly have a "positive thinking", if you hold a negative concept of self. Do you agree? (Para. 8)

____

____

V. Thinking Critically

◇ *Be critical in your thinking.*

◇ *Be skeptical in your thinking.*

◇ *Be introspective in your thinking.*

1. This self-image is our own conception of the "sort of person I am." Do you know the sort of person you are?

____

____

2. But most of these beliefs about ourselves have unconsciously been formed from our past experiences, our successes and failures, our humiliations, our triumphs, and the way other people have reacted to us. How are your past experiences related to your self image?

____

____

3. Have you ever been harassed by the thought that you are not the right person for a particular task? What is it?

____

____

4. Have you ever doubted your ability to do something well? What is it?

____

____

5. The self-image can be changed. What change(s) should you make to establish a more positive self-image?

____

____

6. Do you think your grade in school has had an effect on your self-image?

____

____

7. The point(s) that I do not agree with the writer.

____

____

VI. Thinking Independently

◇ *Develop and form ideas or opinions of your own.*

◇ *Be both inductive and deductive in your thinking.*

◇ *Communicate and share with others.*

◇ *Write and present your composition on one of the following topics.*

1. Self-image—a key to a better life
2. Change the way you look at yourself, and you will change the way you live.
3. My self-image
4. What do I know about myself
5. One thing I am most satisfied with myself
6. One thing I am most unsatisfied with myself
7. One thing I have learned from this passage

Passage 8

WORK

1 Whether work should be placed among the causes of happiness or among the causes of unhappiness may perhaps be regarded as a doubtful question. There is certainly much work which is exceedingly annoying, and an excess of work is always very painful. However, provided work is not excessive in amount, even the dullest work is to most people less painful than idleness. There are in work all grades, from mere relief of tedium up to the profoundest delights, according to the nature of the work and the abilities of the worker.

2 Most of the work that most people have to do is not in itself interesting, but even such work has certain great advantages. To begin with, it fills a good many hours of the day without the need of deciding what one should do. Most people, when they are left free to fill their own time according to their own choice, are at a loss to think of anything sufficiently pleasant to be worth doing. And whatever they decide on, they are troubled by the feeling that some thing else would have been pleasanter. To be able to fill leisure intelligently is the last product of civilization, and at present very few people have reached this level. Moreover the making of choice is in itself tiresome. Except to people with unusual initiative it is positively agreeable to be told what to do at each hour of the day, provided the orders are not too unpleasant. Most of the idle rich suffer unspeakable boredom as the price of their freedom from

drudgery. Accordingly the more intelligent rich men work nearly as hard as if they were poor.

3 Work therefore is desirable, first and foremost, as a preventive of boredom, for the boredom that a man feels when he is doing uninteresting work is nothing in comparison with the boredom that he feels when he has nothing to do with his days. With this advantage of work another is associated, namely that it makes holidays much more delicious when they come.

4 The second advantage of most paid work and of some unpaid work is that it gives chances of success and opportunities for ambition. In most work success is measured by income. It is only where the best work is concerned that this measure ceases to be the natural one to apply. However dull work may be, it becomes bearable if it is a means of building up a reputation, whether in the world at large or only in one's own circle. Continuity of purpose is one of the most essential ingredients of happiness in the long run, and for most men this comes chiefly through their work.

5 Two chief elements make work interesting; first, the exercise of skill, and second, construction.

6 Every man who has acquired some unusual skill enjoys exercising it until it has become a matter of course, or until he can no longer improve himself. Of course there is not only the exercise of kill but the outwitting of a skilled opponent. Even where this competitive element is absent, however, the performance of difficult feats is agreeable. A man who can do stunts in an aeroplane finds the pleasure so great that for the sake of it he is willing to risk his life. All skilled work can be pleasurable, provided the skill required is either variable or capable of indefinite improvement. If these conditions are absent, it will cease to be interesting when a man has acquired his maximum skill. Fortunately there is a very considerable amount of work in which new circumstances call for new skill.

7 There is, however, another element possessed by the best work,

which is even more important as a source of happiness than is the exercise of skill. This is the element of constructiveness. Destruction is of course necessary very often as a preliminary to subsequent construction; in that case it is part of a whole which is constructive. But not infrequently a man will engage in activities of which the purpose is destructive without regard to any construction that may come after. Now I cannot deny that in the work of destruction as in the work of construction there may be joy. It is a fiercer joy, perhaps at moments more intense, but it is less profoundly satisfying, since the result is one in which little satisfaction is to be found. You kill your enemy, and when he is dead your occupation is gone, and the satisfaction that you derive from victory quickly fades. The work of construction, on the other hand, when completed is delightful to contemplate. The most satisfactory purposes are those that lead on indefinitely from one success to another without ever coming to a dead end; and in this respect it will be found that construction is a greater source of happiness than destruction. Perhaps it would be more correct to say that those who find satisfaction in construction find in it greater satisfaction than the lovers of destruction can find in destruction. Few things are likely to cure the habit of hatred. But nothing can rob a man of the happiness of successful achievement in an important piece of work.

8 Great artists and great men of science do work which is in itself delightful; while they are doing it, it secures them the respect from others, which gives them the most fundamental kind of power, namely power over men's thoughts and feelings. They have also the most solid reasons for thinking well of themselves. The combination of these circumstances ought to be enough to make any man happy. Nevertheless it is not so. We cannot maintain that the greatest work must make a man happy; we can only maintain that it must make him less unhappy. Men of science, however, are far less often temperamentally unhappy than artists are.

9 One of the causes of unhappiness among intellectuals in the present day is that so many of them, especially those whose skill is literary, find

no opportunity for the independent exercise of their talents, but have to prostitute their skill to purposes which they believe to be harmful. Such work can no longer derive whole-hearted satisfaction from anything whatever. I cannot condemn men who undertake work of this sort, since starvation is too serious an alternative. But when it is possible to do work that is satisfactory to a man's constructive impulses without entirely starving, he will be well advised to think from the point of his own happiness of work than from the view of being highly paid. Without self-respect genuine happiness is scarcely possible. And the man who is ashamed of his work can hardly achieve self-respect.

10 Human beings differ profoundly in regard to the tendency to regard their lives as a whole. To some men it is natural to do so. To others life is a series of detached incidents without directed movement and without unity. I think the former sort are more likely to achieve happiness than the latter, since they will gradually build up those circumstances from which they can derive self-respect, whereas the others will be blown about by the winds of circumstances now this way, now that, without ever arriving at any haven. The habit of viewing life as a whole is an essential part both of wisdom and of true morality, and is one of the things which ought to be encouraged in education. Consistent purpose is not enough to make life happy, but it is an almost indispensable condition of a happy life. And consistent purpose embodies itself mainly in work.

(By *Bertrand Russell*; Adapted from *An English Reader*)

WORDS AND PHRASES

contemplate【'kɔntempleit】*v.*	look at thoughtfully for a long time
detach *n.*	not attach; separate
drudgery【'dʒʌdʒəri】*n.*	hard and uninteresting work
hierarchy *n.*	formally ranked group
ingredient *n.*	element required for something
stunt *n.*	dangerous feat

I. Understanding the Text

◇ *Understand the subject matter.*

◇ *Read for the main information.*

◇ *Learn the writing technique.*

◇ *Reach the conclusion.*

1. What is the theme of this passage?

____

2. What are the main points made in the passage?

Para. 1: ______________________________

Para. 2 –4: ______________________________

Para. 5 –7: ______________________________

Para. 8 –9: ______________________________

Para. 10: ______________________________

II. Analyzing the Paragraphs

◇ *Summarize the information.*

◇ *Generalize the main idea.*

◇ *Find out the topic sentence.*

1. What is the main idea of Paragraph 1?

____

____

2. What is the main idea of Paragraph 2?

____

____

3. What is the main idea of Paragraph 3?

____

____

4. What is the main idea of Paragraph 4?

____

____

5. What is the main idea of Paragraph 6?

____

____

6. What is the main idea of Paragraph 7?

____

____

7. What is the main idea of Paragraph 8?

____

____

8. What is the main idea of Paragraph 9?

____

____

9. What is the main idea of Paragraph 10?

____

____

III. Learning the Language

◇ *Be aware of and sensitive to language variations and varieties.*

◇ *Choose the language as being used in the passage.*

◇ *Learn the best language.*

1. Whether work should be ________ among the causes of happiness or among the causes of unhappiness may perhaps be regarded as a doubtful question. (Para. 1)

   A) placed B) made C) taken D) considered

2. Provided work is not ________ in amount, even the dullest work is to most people less painful than idleness. (Para. 1)

   A) exceeding B) excessive C) excess D) exceeded

3. Most people, when they are ________ free to fill their own time according to their own choice, are at a loss to think of anything sufficiently pleasant to be worth doing. (Para. 2)

   A) made B) given C) left D) told

4. Work therefore is desirable, first and ________, as a preventive of boredom, for the boredom that a man feels when he is doing uninteresting work is nothing in comparison with the boredom that he feels when he has nothing to do with his days. (Para. 3)
A) most B) last C) after all D) foremost

5. It is only where the best work is concerned that this measure ceases to be the natural one to ________. (Para. 4)
A) apply B) be applied C) use D) be used

6. Every man who has acquired some unusual skill enjoys exercising it until it has become a matter of ________, or until he can no longer improve himself. (Para. 6)
A) cause B) fact C) source D) course

7. You kill your enemy, and when he is dead your occupation is gone, and the satisfaction that you derive from victory quickly ________. (Para. 7)
A) fades B) ceases C) stops D) leaves

8. Great artists and great men of science do work which is in itself delightful; while they are doing it, it ________ them the respect from others, which gives them the most fundamental kind of power, namely power over men's thoughts and feelings. (Para. 8)
A) secures B) guarantees C) saves D) offers

9. Without self-respect ________ happiness is scarcely possible. And the man who is ashamed of his work can hardly achieve self-respect. (Para. 9)
A) factual B) real C) true D) genuine

10. The habit of viewing life as a whole is an essential part ________ wisdom and of true morality, and is one of the things which ought to be encouraged in education. (Para. 10)
A) of both B) both of
C) of either D) either of

IV. Thinking Openly

◇ *Keep your mind open to new ideas.*

◇ *Be receptive to other's opinions.*

◇ *Challenge your own judgment.*

1. Provided work is not excessive in amount, even the dullest work is to most people less painful than idleness. What do you think? (Para. 1)

____

____

2. One advantage of an uninteresting work is that it can fill a good many hours of the day without the need of deciding what one should do. Is that true to you? (Para. 2)

____

____

3. The boredom that a man feels when he is doing uninteresting work is nothing in comparison with the boredom that he feels when he has nothing to do with his days. Do you agree? (Para. 3)

____

____

4. However dull work may be, it becomes bearable if it is a means of building up a reputation. Have you ever thought that way? (Para. 4)

____

____

5. Continuity of purpose is one of the most essential ingredients of happiness in the long run, and for most men this comes chiefly through their work. Can that be true for most women? (Para. 4)

____

____

6. The joy in the work of destruction is fiercer, perhaps at moments more intense, but it is less profoundly satisfying, since the result is one in which little satisfaction is to be found. What is your

viewpoint? (Para. 7)

7. Perhaps it would be more correct to say that those who find satisfaction in construction find in it greater satisfaction than the lovers of destruction can find in destruction. What do you think? (Para. 7)

8. Great artists and great men of science do work which gives them the most fundamental kind of power, namely power over men's thoughts and feelings. Do you agree or not? (Para. 8)

9. Without self-respect genuine happiness is scarcely possible. And the man who is ashamed of his work can hardly achieve self-respect. What is your opinion? (Para. 9)

10. The habit of viewing life as a whole is an essential part both of wisdom and of true morality, and is one of the things which ought to be encouraged in education. Why? (Para. 10)

V. Thinking Critically

◇ *Be critical in your thinking.*

◇ *Be introspective of yourself.*

◇ *Understand the kind of person you are.*

1. What kind of work is exceedingly annoying to you?

2. Most people, when they are left free to fill their own time according to their own choice, are at a loss to think of anything sufficiently pleasant to be worth doing. Does this apply to you?

____

____

3. Except to people with unusual initiative it is positively agreeable to be told what to do at each hour of the day, provided the orders are not too unpleasant. Are you such a person?

____

____

4. It is only where the best work is concerned that income ceases to be a natural measure to apply. What is your measure of the best work?

____

____

5. Every man who has acquired some unusual skill enjoys exercising it. What skill do you have in enjoying exercising?

____

____

6. Have you ever engaged in an activity of which the purpose is destructive without regard to any construction that may come after?

____

____

7. What do you think is the thing that is likely to cure the habit of hatred?

____

____

8. What is the work that you can find an opportunity for the independent exercise of your talents?

____

____

9. Do you have the tendency to regard life as a whole or rather as a series

of detached incidents without directed movement and unity?

____

____

10. The point(s) that I do not agree with the writer.

____

____

VI. Thinking Independently

◇ *Develop and form ideas or opinions of your own.*

◇ *Be both inductive and deductive in your thinking.*

◇ *Communicate and share with others.*

◇ *Write and present your composition on one of the following topics.*

1. Work and happiness
2. The work that I mostly desire to do
3. What does work mean to me?
4. Work and play
5. One thing I have Learned from this passage

Passage 9

ON FRIENDSHIP

1 Few Americans stay put for a lifetime. We move from town to city to suburb, from high school to college in a different state, from a job in one region to a better job elsewhere, from the home where we raise our children to the home where we plan to live in retirement. With each move we are forever making new friends, who become part of our new life at that time.

2 For many of us the summer is a special time for forming new friendships. Today millions of Americans vacation abroad, and they go not only to see new sights but also with the hope of meeting new people. No one really expects a vacation trip to produce a close friend. But surely the beginning of a friendship is possible. Surely in every country people value friendship.

3 The difficulty when strangers from two countries meet is not a lack of appreciation of friendship, but different expectations about what constitutes friendship and how it comes into being. In those European countries that Americans are most likely to visit, friendship is quite sharply distinguished from other, more casual relations, and is differently related to family life. For a Frenchman, a German or an Englishman friendship is usually more particularized and carries a heavier burden of commitment.

4 But as we use the word, "friend" can be applied to a wide range of relationship—to someone one has known for a few weeks in a new place, to a close business associate, to a childhood playmate, to a man or woman, to a trusted confidant. There are real differences among these relations for Americans—a friendship may be superficial, casual, situational or deep and enduring. But to a European, who sees only our surface behavior, the differences are not clear.

5 Who, then, is a friend? Even simple translation from one language to another is difficult. "You see," a Frenchman explains, "if I were to say to you in France, 'This is my good friend,' that person would not be as close to me as someone about whom I said only, 'This is my friend.' Anyone about whom I have to say more is really less."

6 For the French, friendship is a one-to-one relationship that demands a keen awareness of the other person's intellect, temperament and particular interests. A friend is someone who draws out your own best qualities, with whom you sparkle and become more of whatever the friendship draws upon. Your political philosophy assumes more depth, appreciation of a play becomes sharper, taste in food or wine is made more noticeable, and enjoyment of a sport is intensified.

7 And French friendships are compartmentalized. A man may play chess with a friend for thirty years without knowing his political opinions, or he may talk politics with him for as long a time without knowing about his personal life. Different friends fill different positions in each person's life. These friendships are not made part of family life. A friend is not expected to spend evenings being nice to children or courteous to a deaf grandmother. These duties, also serious and enjoyed, are primarily for relatives. Men who are friends may meet in a café. Intellectual friends may meet in large groups for evenings of conversation. Working people may meet at the little bar where they drink and talk, far from the family. Marriage does not affect such friendships; wives do not have to be taken into account.

8 In the past in France, friendships of this kind seldom were open to any but intellectual women. Since most women's lives centered on their homes, their warmest relations with other women often went back to their girlhood. The special relationship of friendship is based on what the French value most—on the mind, on compatibility of outlook, on vivid awareness of some chosen area of life.

9 In Germany, in contrast with France, friendship is much more articulately a matter of feeling. Adolescents, boys and girls, form deeply sentimental attachments, walk and talk together—not so much to polish their wits as to share hopes and fears and dreams, to form a common front against the world of school and family and to join in a kind of mutual discovery of each other's and their own inner life. Within the family, the closest relationship over a lifetime is between brothers and sisters. Outside the family, men and women find in their closest friends of the same sex the devotion of a sister, the loyalty of a brother. Appropriately, in Germany friends usually are brought into the family. Children call their father's and their mother's friends "uncle" and "aunt." Between French friends, who have chosen each other for the congeniality of their point of view, lively disagreement and sharpness of argument are the breath of life. But for Germans, whose friendships are based on mutuality of feelings, deep disagreement on any subject that matters to both is regarded as a tragedy. Like ties of kinship, ties of friendship are meant to be unalterably binding. Young Germans who come to the United States have great difficulty in establishing such friendships with Americans. We view friendship more tentatively, subject to change in intensity as people move, change their job, marry, or discover new interest.

10 English friendships follow still a different pattern. Their basis is shared activity. Activities at different stages of life may be of very different kinds—discovering a common interest in school, serving together in the armed forces, taking part in a foreign mission, staying in the same country house during a crisis. In the midst of the activity, whatever it

maybe, people fall into step—sometimes two men or two women, sometimes two couples, sometimes three people—and find that they walk or play a game or tell stories or serve on a tiresome committee with the same easy anticipation of what each will do day by day or in some critical situation. Americans who have made English friends comment that, even years later, "you can take up just where you left off." Meeting after a long interval, friends are like a couple who begin to dance again when the orchestra strikes up after a pause. English friends are formed outside the family circle, but they are not, as in Germany, contrapuntal to the family nor are they, as in France, separated from the family. And a break in an English friendship comes not necessarily as a result of some irreconcilable difference of viewpoint or feeling but instead as a result of misjudgment, where one friend seriously misjudges how the other will think or feel or act, so that suddenly they are out of step.

11 What, then, is friendship? Looking at these different styles, including our own, each of which is related to a whole way of life, are there common elements? There is the recognition that friendship, in contrast with kinship, invokes freedom of choice. A friend is someone who chooses and is chosen. And between friends there is inevitably a kind of equality of give-and-take. These similarities make the bridge between societies possible, and the American's characteristic openness to different styles of relationship makes it possible for him to find new friends abroad with whom he feels at home.

WORDS AND PHRASES

articulately *adv.*	spoken or expressed clearly
binding[ˈbaindiŋ] *adj.*	having power to hold one to an agreement
compartmentalize [kəmpaːtˈmentəlaiz] *v.*	divide things into separate parts
compatibility [kəmˌpætəˈbiləti] *n.*	the ability to exist/live/work with sb. else

confidant【ˈkɔnfidænt】*n.*	a person trusted
congeniality【kənˌdʒiːniˈæliti】*n.*	the same or similar nature
contrapuntal【ˌkɔntrəˈpʌntl】*adj.*	relating to or marked by counterpoint
draw out	cause to come out
draw upon	make use of
irreconcilable【iˌrekənˈsailəbl】*adj.*	impossible to find agreement between/with
leave off	stop doing something
out of step	not move or agree at the same rate
stay put	stay in place
strike up	start to play or sing
temperament【ˈtemprəmənt】*n.*	a person's nature
tentatively【ˈtentətivli】*adv.*	by way of a test
the breath of life	the most important thing in one's life

I. Understanding the Text

◇ *Understand the subject matter.*

◇ *Read for the main information.*

◇ *Learn the writing technique.*

◇ *Reach the conclusion.*

1. What is the theme of this passage?

____

2. What peoples' friendships are being talked about in this passage?

Para. 1 –4: ______________________________

Para. 5 –8: ______________________________

Para. 9: ______________________________

Para. 10: ______________________________

3. What conclusions are drawn in this passage?

Pra. 11 ______________________________

II. Analyzing the Paragraphs

◇ *Summarize the information.*

◇ *Generalize the main idea.*

◇ *Find out the topic sentence.*

Part One: AMERICAN FRIENDSHIP

1. What is the main idea of Paragraph 1?

____

2. What is the main idea of Paragraph 2?

____

3. What is the main idea of Paragraph 3?

____

4. What is the main idea of Paragraph 4?

____

Part Two: FRENCH FRIENDSHIP

5. What is the main idea of Paragraph 5?

____

6. What is the main idea of Paragraph 6?

____

7. What is the main idea of Paragraph 7?

____

8. What is the main idea of Paragraph 8?

____

Part Three: GERMAN FRIENDSHIP

9. What is the main idea of Paragraph 9?

____

Part Four: ENGLISH FRIENDSHIP

10. What is the main idea of Paragraph 10?

____

Part Five: SUMMARY

11. What is the main idea of Paragraph 11?

____

III. Learning the Language

◇ *Be aware of and sensitive to language variations and varieties.*

◇ *Choose the language as being used in the passage.*

◇ *Learn the best language.*

1. Few Americans ________ for a lifetime. We move from town to city to suburb and from high school to college in a different state. (Para. 1)

   A) stay put　B) put stay　C) stay up　D) stay out

2. For many of us the summer is a special time for ________ new friendships. (Para. 2)

   A) growing　B) forming　C) making　D) creating

3. For the French, friendship is a ________ relationship that demands a keen awareness of the other person's intellect, temperament and particular interests. (Para. 6)

   A) one-with-one　B) one-for-one
   C) one-to-one　D) one-on-one

4. Your political philosophy assumes more depth, appreciation of a play ________, taste in food or wine is made more noticeable, and enjoyment of a sport is intensified. (Para. 6)

   A) made sharp　B) made sharper
   C) becomes sharp　D) becomes sharper

5. In the past in France, friendships of this kind seldom were open ________ but intellectual women. (Para. 8)

   A) to any　B) to some　C) to no one　D) to all

6. In Germany, ________ France, friendship is much more articulately a matter of feeling. (Para. 9)

   A) in contrast to　B) in contrast with
   C) by contrast to　D) by contrast with

7. Between French friends, who have chosen each other for the congeniality of their point of view, lively disagreement and sharpness of argument are ________. (Para. 9)

   A) the breath of life　B) the breath of living

C) the breath of a life D) the breath of a living

8. English friendships follow still a different pattern. Their ________. (Para. 10)

A) base is shared activity B) base is a shared activity

C) basis is shared activity D) basis is a shared activity

9. Meeting after a long interval, friends are like a couple who begin to dance again when the orchestra ________ after a pause. (Para. 10)

A) strikes out B) strikes on

C) strikes off D) strikes up

10. English friends are formed outside the family circle, but they are not, as in Germany, ________ the family nor are they, as in France, separated from the family. (Para. 10)

A) compatible to B) congenial to

C) contrapuntal to D) subject to

IV. Thinking Openly

◇ *Keep your mind open to new ideas.*

◇ *Be receptive to other's opinions.*

◇ *Challenge your own judgment.*

1. The difficulty when strangers from two countries meet is not a lack of appreciation of friendship, but different expectations about what constitutes friendship and how it comes into being. Do you agree? (Para. 3)

____

____

2. For a Frenchman, a German or an Englishman friendship is usually particularized and caries a heavier burden of commitment. What's your comment? (Para 3)

____

____

3. American friendship may be superficial, casual, situational or deep

and enduring. Why? Give your reasons. (Para. 4)

4. The special relationship of (French) friendship is based on what the French value most—on the mind, on compatibility of outlook, on vivid awareness of some chosen area of life. Is friendship a reflection of one's value? (Para. 8)

V. Thinking Critically

◇ *Be critical in your thinking.*

◇ *Be skeptical in your thinking.*

◇ *Be introspective in your thinking.*

1. Which of the following is Chinese friendship like most, American friendship, French friendship, German friendship, or English friendship?

2. How do you characterize Chinese friendship?

3. What is it that is most likely to end our Chinese friendship?

4. And between friends there is inevitably a kind of equality of give-and-take. What do you "give" to your friends and what do you "take" from them?

5. Friendship is related to one's way of life. Do you agree? In what way is

friendship related to your way of life?

VI. Thinking Independently

◇ *Develop and form ideas or opinions of your own.*

◇ *Be both inductive and deductive in your thinking.*

◇ *Communicate and share with others.*

◇ *Write and present your composition on one of the following topics.*

1. On friendship
2. A friend in need is a friend indeed.
3. What does friendship mean to me?
4. The equality of give-and-take between friends
5. Things I can give to my friends
6. Things I want to have from my friends
7. One thing I have learned from this passage

Passage 10

HOW TO CHALLENGE YOUR POINT OF VIEW

1 Dr. Edward Jenner was busy trying to solve the problem of smallpox. After studying case after case, he still found no possible cure. He had reached an impasse in his thinking. At this point, he changed his tactics. Instead of focusing on people who had smallpox, he switched his attention to people who did not have smallpox. It turned out that dairymaids apparently never got the disease. From the discovery that harmless cowpox gave protection against deadly smallpox came vaccination and the end of smallpox as a scourge in the western world.

2 We often reach an impasse in our thinking. We are looking at a problem and trying to solve it and it seems there is a dead end. It is on these occasions that we become tense, we feel pressured, overwhelmed, in a state of stress. We struggle vainly, fighting to solve the problem.

3 Dr. Jenner, however, did something about this situation. He stopped fighting the problem and simply changed his point of view—from his patients to dairy maids. Picture the process going something like this: Suppose the brain is computer. This computer has absorbed into its memory bank all your history, your experiences, your training, your information received through life; and it is programmed according to all

this data. To change your point of view, you must reprogram your computer, thus freeing yourself to take in new ideas and develop new ways of looking at things. Dr. Jenner, in effect, by reprogramming his computer, erased the old way of looking at his smallpox problem and was free to receive new alternatives.

4 That's all very well, you may say, but how do we actually do that?

5 Doctor and philosopher Edward de Bono has come up with a technique for changing our point of view, and he calls it Lateral Thinking.

6 The normal Western approach to a problem is to fight it. The saying, "When the going gets tough, the tough gets going," is typical of this aggressive attitude toward problem-solving. No matter what the problem is, or the techniques available for solving it, the framework produced by our Western way of thinking is fight. Dr. de Bono calls this vertical thinking; the traditional, sequential, Aristotelian thinking of logic, moving firmly from one step to the next, like toy blocks being built on top of the other. The flaw is, of course, that if at any point one of the steps is not reached, or one of the toy blocks is incorrectly placed, then the whole structure collapses. Impasse is reached, and frustration, tension, feelings of fight take over.

7 Lateral thinking, Dr. de Bono says, is a new technique of thinking about things—a technique that avoids this fight altogether, and solves the problem in an entirely unexpected fashion.

8 In one of Sherlock Holmes's cases, his assistant, Dr. Watson, pointed out that a certain dog was of no importance to the case because it did not appear to have done anything. Sherlock Holmes took the opposite point of view and maintained that the fact the dog had done nothing was of the utmost significance, for it should have been expected to do something, and on this basis he solved the case.

9 Lateral thinking sounds simple. And it is. Once you have solved a problem laterally, you wonder how you could ever have been hung up on it. The key is making that vital shift in emphasis, that sidestepping of the

problem, instead of attacking it head-on.

10 Dr. A. A. Bridger, psychiatrist at Columbia University and in private practice in New York, explains how lateral thinking works with his patients. "Many people come to me wanting to stop smoking, for instance," he says. "Most people fail when they are trying to stop smoking because they wind up telling themselves, "No, I will not smoke; no, I shall not smoke; no, I will not; no, I cannot…" It's a fight and what happens is you end up smoking more."

11 "So instead of looking at the problem from the old ways of no, and fighting it, I show them a whole new point of view—that you are your body's keeper, and your body is something through which you experience life. If you stop to think about it, there's really something helpless about your body. It can do nothing for itself. It has no choice; it is like a baby's body. You begin then a whole new way of looking at it—I am now going to take care of myself, and give myself some respect and protection, by not smoking.

12 There is a Japanese parable about a donkey tied to a pole by a rope. The rope rubs tight against his neck. The more the donkey fights and pulls on the rope, the tighter and tighter it gets around his throat-until he winds up dead. On the other hand, as soon as he stops fighting, he finds that the rope gets slack, he can walk around; maybe find some grass to eat… That's the same principle: The more you fight something the more anxious you become; the more you're involved in a bad pattern, the more difficult it is to escape pain.

13 "Lateral thinking," Dr. Bridger goes on, "is simply approaching a problem with what I would call an Eastern flanking maneuver. You know, when a zen archer wants to hit the target with a bow and arrow, he doesn't concentrate on the target, he concentrates rather on what he has in his hands, so when he lets the arrow go, his focus is on the arrow, rather than the target. This is what an Eastern flanking maneuver implies—instead of approaching the target directly, you approach it from a sideways point of view—or laterally instead of vertically."

14 "I think the answer lies in that direction," affirms Dr. Bridger. Take the situation where someone is in a crisis. The Chinese word for crisis is divided into two characters, one meaning danger and the other meaning opportunity. We in the Western world focus only upon the 'danger' aspect of crisis. Crisis in Western civilization has come to mean danger, period. And yet the word can also mean opportunity. Let us now suggest to the person in crisis that he ceases concentrating upon the dangers involved and the difficulties, and concentrates instead upon the opportunity—for there is always opportunity in crisis. Looking at a crisis from an opportunity point of view is a lateral thought.

WORDS AND PHRASES

cowpox【'kaupɔks】*n.*	牛痘
erase【i'reiz】*v.*	rub out; scrape out
flank【flæŋk】*v.*	attack the side of
going【'gəuiŋ】*n.*	conditions for progress
head-on *adv.*	in a direct manner
impasse【'mpæs】*n.*	a position from which progress is impossible
maneuver【mə'nu:və】*n.*	a skillful move/trick
parable【'pærəbl】*n.*	a brief story to teach some moral lesson/truth
scourge【skə:dʒ】*n.*	thing or person that causes great trouble/misfortune
slack【slæk】*adj.*	loose; not tight; not firm
smallpox【'smɔ:lpɔks】*n.*	a contagious disease causing spots on the skin
vaccination【ˌvæksi'neiʃn】*n.*	接种疫苗
Zen【zen;zɛn】*n.*	emphasizing the value of meditation and intuition

I. Understanding the Text

◇ *Understand the subject matter.*

◇ *Read for the main information.*

◇ *Learn the writing technique.*

◇ *Reach the conclusion.*

1. What is the theme of this passage?

____

2. What are the main points made in the passage?

   Para. 1 – 3: ______________________________

   Para. 4 – 5: ______________________________

   Para. 6 – 8: ______________________________

   Para. 9 – 14: ______________________________

II. Analyzing the Paragraphs

◇ *Summarize the information.*

◇ *Generalize the main idea.*

◇ *Find out the topic sentence.*

1. What is the main idea of Paragraph 1?

____

2. Why does the author talk about Dr. Edward Jenner's discovery at the beginning of the passage? (Para. 1)

____

3. What is the main idea of Paragraph 2?

____

4. What is the main idea of Paragraph 3?

____

5. What does the writer want to tell us with the analogy between our human brain and computer? (Para. 3)

____

6. What is the main idea of Paragraph 6?

____

7. What is the main idea of Paragraph 7?

____

8. What is the main idea of Paragraph 8?

____

9. What is the main idea of Paragraph 9?

____

10. What is the main idea of Paragraph 10 and 11?

____

11. What is the main idea of Paragraph 12?

____

12. What is the main idea of Paragraph 13?

____

13. What is the main idea of Paragraph 14?

____

III. Learning the Language

◇ *Be aware of and sensitive to language variations and varieties.*

◇ *Choose the language as being used in the passage.*

◇ *Learn the best language.*

1. After studying case after case, he still ________ possible cure. (Para. 1)
   A) didn't find any　　B) found no
   C) found out no　　D) founded no
2. Instead of focusing on people who had smallpox, he _____ his attention to people who did not have smallpox. (Para. 1)
   A) switched　　B) exchanged　　C) returned　　D) adjusted
3. Dr. Jenner, in effect, by reprogramming his computer, erased the old way of looking at his smallpox problem and was free to receive new ________. (Para. 3)
   A) choice　　B) choices　　C) alternative　　D) alternatives
4. The normal Western approach to a problem is to fight it. The saying,

"When the going gets tough, the tough gets going," is ________ this aggressive attitude toward problem-solving. (Para. 6)

A) capable of　　B) characteristic of

C) typical of　　D) representative of

5. Impasse is reached, and frustration, tension, feelings of fight ________. (Para. 6)

A) take on　　B) take over

C) take in　　D) take out

6. Once you have solved a problem laterally, you wonder how you could ever have been ________ on it. (Para. 9)

A) hung back　　B) hung in

C) hung up　　D) hung about

7. Dr. A. Bridger, psychiatrist at Columbia University and in private practice in New York, explains how lateral thinking ________ his patients. (Para. 10)

A) works to　　B) works in

C) works for　　D) works with

8. The key is making that vital shift in emphasis, that ________ of the problem, instead of attacking it head-on. (Para. 9)

A) sidestepping　　B) side step

C) stepping aside　　D) step aside

9. Let us now suggest to the person in crisis that he ________ upon the dangers involved and the difficulties, and concentrate instead upon the opportunity-for there is always opportunity in crisis. (Para. 14)

A) ceases concentrating　　B) cease concentrating

C) cease to concentrate　　D) ceases in concentrating

10. Looking at a crisis from ________ point of view is a lateral thought. (Para. 14)

A) that opportunity　　B) opportunity

C) the opportunity　　D) an opportunity

IV. Thinking Openly

◇ *Keep your mind open to new ideas.*

◇ *Be receptive to other's opinions.*

◇ *Challenge your own judgment.*

1. The normal Western approach to a problem is to fight it. What do you think is our Chinese approach to a problem? (Para. 6)

____

____

2. The saying, "When the going gets tough, the tough gets going," is typical of this (American) aggressive attitude toward problem-solving. What is your attitude toward problem-solving? (Para. 6)

____

____

3. Dr. de Bono calls this vertical thinking the traditional, sequential, Aristotelian thinking of logic. Can you come to a Chinese philosopher, whose thinking you would like to talk about? (Para. 6)

____

____

4. The more you fight something the more anxious you become—the more you're involved in a bad pattern, the more difficult it is to escape pain. Do you have a similar experience? (Para. 12)

____

____

5. Judging from the Japanese parable in Para. 12, what do you think is the Japanese way of thinking, vertical or lateral?

____

____

V. Thinking Critically

◇ *Be critical in your thinking.*

◇ *Be skeptical in your thinking.*

◇ *Be introspective in your thinking.*

1. The passage implies that vertical thinking is typically the Western way of thinking while lateral thinking is the Eastern way of thinking. Do you agree? What do you think is your way of thinking?

___

___

2. Can you come up with more examples such as '危机' to further exemplify the Chinese culture and the way of our thinking as well?

___

___

3. Have you ever solved a problem by changing your way of thinking? What is it?

___

___

4. Is it possible that one thinks both vertically and laterally? If yes, which, do you think, should come first? Why?

___

___

5. The point(s) that I do not agree with the writer.

___

___

VI. Thinking Independently

◇ *Develop and form ideas or opinions of your own.*

◇ *Be both inductive and deductive in your thinking.*

◇ *Communicate and share with others.*

◇ *Write and present your composition on one of the following topics.*

1. On thinking
2. My way of developing my thinking skills

3. Creativity requires creative thinking
4. How to think creatively
5. The way I've solved a problem by thinking differently
6. One thing I have learned from this passage

Passage 11

BORN TO WIN

1 Each human being is born as something new, something that never existed before. He is born with what he needs to win at life. Each person in his own way can see, hear, touch, taste, and think for himself. Each has his unique potentials—his capabilities and limitations. Each can be a significant, thinking, aware, and creatively productive person in his own right—a winner.

2 The words "winner" and "loser" have many meanings. When we refer to a person as a winner, we do not mean one who beats the other guy by winning over him and making him lose. To us, a winner is one who responds authentically by being credible, trustworthy, responsive, and genuine, both as an individual and as a member of a society. A loser is one who fails to correspond authentically. Martin Buber[1] expresses this idea as he retells an old story of a rabbi[2] who on his death bed sees himself as a loser. The rabbi laments that, in the world to come, he will not be asked why he wasn't Moses[3], he will be asked why he wasn't himself.

3 Few people are one hundred percent winners or one hundred percent losers. It's a matter of degree. However, once a person is on the road to being a winner, his chances are greater for becoming even more so. This

book is intended to facilitate the journey.

4 Winners have different potentials. Achievement is not the most important thing. Authenticity is. The authentic person experiences the reality of himself by knowing himself, being himself, and becoming a credible, responsive person. He actualizes his own unprecedented uniqueness and appreciates the uniqueness of others. (The common pronoun "he" refers to persons of either sex except when "she" is definitely applicable.)

5 A winner is not afraid to do his own thinking and to use his own knowledge. He can separate facts from opinion and doesn't pretend to have all the answers. While he can admire and respect other people, he is not totally defined, bound, or awed by them.

6 A winner can be spontaneous. He does not have to respond in predetermined, rigid ways. He can change his plans when the situation calls for it. A winner has a zest for life. He enjoys work, play, food, other people, and the world of nature. Without guilt he enjoys his own accomplishments. Without envy he enjoys the accomplishments of others.

7 Although a winner can freely enjoy himself, he can also postpone enjoyment. He can discipline himself in the present to enhance his enjoyment in the future. He is not afraid to go after what he wants but does so in appropriate ways. He does not get his security by controlling others.

8 A winner cares about the world and its peoples. He is not isolated from the general problems of society. He is concerned, compassionate and committed to improving the quality of life. Even in the face of national and international adversity, he does not see himself as totally powerless. He does what he can to make the world a better place.

9 Although people are born to win, they are also born helpless and totally dependent on their environment. Winners successfully make the transition from total helplessness to independence, and then to interdependence. Losers do not. Somewhere along the line they begin to avoid becoming self-responsible.

10 As we have noted, few people are total winners or losers. Most of them are winners in some areas of their lives and losers in others. Their winning or losing is influenced by what happens to them in childhood.

11 A lack of response to dependency needs, poor nutrition, brutality, unhappy relationships, disease, continuing disappointments, inadequate physical care, and traumatic events are among the many experiences that contribute to making people losers. Such experiences interrupt, deter, or prevent the normal progress toward autonomy and self-actualization. To cope with negative experiences a child learns to manipulate himself and others. These manipulative techniques are hard to give up later in life and often become set patterns. A winner works to shed them. A loser hangs on to them.

12 A loser represses his capacity to express spontaneously and appropriately his full range of possible behavior. He may be unaware of other options for his life if the path he chooses goes nowhere. He is afraid to try new things. He maintains his own status quo. He is a repeater. He repeats not only his own mistakes; he often repeats those of his family and culture.

13 A loser has difficulty giving and receiving affection. He dose not enter into intimate, honest direct relationships with others. Instead, he tries to manipulate them into living up to his expectations and channels his energies into living up to their expectations.

14 When a person wants to discover and change his "losing streak", when he wants to become more like the winner he was born to be, he can use gestalt-type experiments and transactional analysis[4] to make change happen. These are two new, exciting, psychological approaches to human problems. The first was given new life by Dr. Frederick Perls; the second was developed by Dr. Eric Berne.

15 Perls was born in Germany in 1893 and left the country when Hitler came into power. Berne was born in Montreal in 1910. Both men were trained as Freudian psychoanalysts; both broke away from the use of

orthodox psychoanalysis; both found their greatest popularity and acceptance in the United States.

16 Gestalt therapy[5] is not new. However, its current popularity has grown very rapidly since it was given new impetus and direction by Dr. Frederick Perls. Gestalt is a German word for which there is no exact English equivalent; it means, roughly, the forming of an organized, meaningful whole.

17 Perls perceives many personalities as lacking wholeness, as being fragmented. He claims people are often aware of only parts of themselves rather than of the whole self. For example, a woman may not know or want to admit that sometimes she acts like her mother; a man may not know or admit that sometimes he wants to cry like a baby.

18 The aim of gestalt therapy is to help one to become—to help the person become aware of, admit to, reclaim, and integrate his fragmented parts. Integration helps a person make the transition from dependency to self-sufficiency; from authoritarian outer support to authentic inner support.

(By *Muriel James* and *Dorothy Jongeward*)

WORDS AND PHRASES

adversity[əd'və:səti] *n.*	misfortune; misery
authentically[ɔ:θentikli] *adv.*	sincerely
channel *v.*	guide/send through a channel
compassionate[kəm'pæʃənət] *adj.*	sympathetic
impetus['impitəs] *n.*	a driving force
in one's own right	through one's own authority or ability
lament[lə'ment] *v.*	regret deeply
manipulate[mə'nipjuleit] *v.*	handle with skill
option['ɔpʃn] *n.*	choice
orthodox['ɔ:θədɔks] *adj.*	holding the accepted beliefs
repress[ri'pres] *v.*	beat down; suppress

rigid【'ridʒid】*adj.* stiff; firm
spontaneous【spɔn'teinjəs】*adj.* self-starting
status quo <拉>现状
streak【stri:k】*n.* a slight tendency, esp. in contrast with one's general character
traumatic【trɔ:mætik】*adj.* startling; shocking
zest【zest】*n.* enthusiasm

Notes on the Text

[1] Martin Buber (1878 – 1965): Austrian-born Judaic (犹太教的) scholar and philosopher

[2] rabbi: 拉比（犹太教负责执行教规、律法并主持宗教仪式的人员）

[3] Moses: in the Bible, the law giver and founder of the Hebrew nation. He led the Israelites out of bondage in Egypt, and during the wandering in the wilderness molded them into a religious and political unity.

[4] Transactional analysis: a form of psychoanalysis that deals with various levels on which a person functions in his relation to others and attempts to integrate or harmonize these levels within the personality

[5] Gestalt therapy: a form of psychological therapy stressing the unity of any body

I. Understanding the Text

◇ *Understand the subject matter.*

◇ *Read for the main information.*

◇ *Learn the writing technique.*

◇ *Reach the conclusion.*

1. What is the theme of this passage?

____

2. What are the main points made in the passage?

   Para. 1 – 3: ____________________

   Para. 4 – 8: ____________________

   Para. 9 – 13: ____________________

   Para. 14 – 18: ____________________

II. Analyzing the Paragraphs

◇ *Summarize the information.*

◇ *Generalize the main idea.*

◇ *Find out the topic sentence.*

WHAT DO WE MEAN BY WINNERS AND LOSERS?

1. Which is the topic sentence of Paragraph 1?

   ____

2. Which is the topic sentence of Paragraph 2?

   ____

3. Which is the topic sentence of Paragraph 3?

   ____

WINNERS

4. What are the potentials that winners have?

   Para. 4: ____________________

   Para. 5: ____________________

   Para. 6: ____________________

   Para. 7: ____________________

   Para. 8: ____________________

WHAT MAKES PEOPLE WINNERS OR LOSERS?

5. What is the main idea of Paragraph 9?

   ____

6. What is the main idea of Paragraph 10?

   ____

7. What is the main idea of Paragraph 11?

   ____

LOSERS

8. What are the problems with losers?

Para. 12: ____________________

Para. 13: ____________________

APPROACHES TO CHANGE ONE'S "LOSING STREAK"

9. What is the main idea of Paragraph 14?

____

10. What is the main idea of Paragraph 15?

____

11. What is the main idea of Paragraph 16?

____

12. What is the main idea of Paragraph 17?

____

13. What is the main idea of Paragraph 18?

____

III. Learning the Language

◇ *Be aware of and sensitive to language variations and varieties.*

◇ *Choose the language as being used in the passage.*

◇ *Learn the best language.*

1. Each can be a significant, thinking, aware, and creatively productive person ________ his own right—a winner. (Para. 1)

   A) in　　B) with　　C) on　　D) for

2. When we refer to a person as a winner, we do not mean one who beats the other guy by ________ him and making him lose. (Para. 2)

   A) winning　　B) winning over　　C) gaining　　D) gaining over

3. Few people are one hundred percent winners or one hundred percent losers. It's a matter of ________. (Para. 3)

   A) fact　　B) course　　C) extent　　D) degree

4. A winner is not afraid ________ his own thinking and to use his own knowledge. He can separate facts from opinion and doesn't pretend to

have all the answers. (Para. 5)

A) to make B) to do C) to utilize D) to take

5. A winner can be spontaneous. He does not have to respond in predetermined, rigid ways. He can change his plans when the situation ________ it. (Para. 6)

A) asks for B) asks C) calls for D) calls

6. He is not afraid to ________ what he wants but does so in appropriate ways. (Para. 7)

A) go on B) go for C) go after D) go with

7. A winner is not isolated from the general problems of society. He is concerned, ________ and committed to improving the quality of life. (Para. 8)

A) compassionate B) compassion

C) passionate D) pathetic

8. Even in the face of national and international ________, he does not see himself as totally powerless. (Para. 8)

A) adverse B) adversity C) adversary D) perversity

9. These manipulative techniques are hard to give up later in life and often become ________. A winner works to shed them. A loser hangs on to them. (Para. 11)

A) patterns fixed B) patterns set

C) fixed patterns D) set patterns

10. A loser ________ his capacity to express spontaneously and appropriately his full range of possible behavior. (Para. 12)

A) compresses B) depresses C) represses D) oppresses

IV. Thinking Openly

◇ *Keep your mind open to new ideas.*

◇ *Be receptive to other's opinions.*

◇ *Challenge your own judgment.*

1. Each human being is born as something new, something that never

existed before. Is this the way you look at yourself? (Para. 1)

2. Few people are one hundred percent winners or one hundred percent losers. It's a matter of degree. What is your viewpoint? (Para. 3)

3. However, once a person is on the road to being a winner, his chances are greater for becoming even more so. Do you agree? How do you know whether a person is on the road to being a winner or not? (Para. 3)

4. Although a winner can freely enjoy himself, he can also postpone enjoyment. What's your comment? (Para. 7)

5. A winner does not see himself as totally powerless. He does what he can to make the world a better place. What do you think? (Para. 8)

6. Winners successfully make the transition from total helplessness to independence, and then to interdependence. What do you want to say about this transition? (Para. 9)

7. A loser is a repeater. He repeats not only his own mistakes; he often repeats those of his family and culture. Are you sometimes a repeater? What mistakes are you more likely to repeat? (Para. 12)

V. Thinking Critically

◇ *Be critical in your thinking.*

◇ *Be skeptical in your thinking.*

◇ *Be introspective in your thinking.*

1. A winner actualizes his own unprecedented uniqueness and appreciates the uniqueness of others. Do you think you are a person who appreciates the uniqueness of others?

____

____

2. He can separate facts from opinion. What is the importance of separating facts from opinion?

____

____

3. A winner has a zest for life. He enjoys work, play, food, other people, and the world of nature. Do you think you are such a person?

____

____

4. Without guilt he enjoys his own accomplishments. Without envy a winner enjoys the accomplishments of others. Can you do so?

____

____

5. A winner is concerned, compassionate and committed to improving the quality of life. To you, what is the quality of life?

____

____

6. Most of them are winners in some areas of their lives and losers in others. In what areas are you a winner and a loser in others?

____

____

7. A loser has difficulty giving and receiving affection. Do you have this

difficulty?

____

____

8. The point(s) that I do not agree with the writer.

____

____

VI. Thinking Independently

◇ *Develop and form ideas or opinions of your own.*

◇ *Be both inductive and deductive in your thinking.*

◇ *Communicate and share with others.*

◇ *Write and present your composition on one of the following topics.*

1. On success
2. The kind of person I want to become
3. My potentials and limitations
4. My childhood dream is still alive.
5. The qualities needed to be a winner
6. One thing I have learned from this passage

Passage 12

BEAUTY

1 For the Greeks, beauty was a virtue: a kind of excellence. Persons then were assumed to be what we now have to call—lamely, enviously—whole persons. If it did not occur to the Greeks to distinguish between a person's "inside" and "outside," they still expected that inner beauty would be matched by beauty of the other kind. The well-born young Athenians who gathered around Socrates found it quite paradoxical that their hero was so intelligent, so brave, so honorable, so seductive and so ugly. One of Socrates' main pedagogical acts was to the ugly—teach those innocent, no doubt splendid-looking disciples of his how full of paradoxes life really was.

2 They may have resisted Socrates' lesson. We do not. Several thousand years later, we are more cautious about the enchantments of beauty. We not only split off—with the greatest facility—the "inside" (character, intellect) from the "outside" (looks); but we are actually surprised when someone who is beautiful is also intelligent, talented, good.

3 It was principally that influence of Christianity that deprived beauty of the central place it had in classical ideals of human excellence. By limiting excellence (virtus in Latin) to moral virtue only, Christianity set beauty adrift —as an alienated, arbitrary, superficial enchantment. And beauty has continued to lose prestige. For close to two centuries it has become a convention to attribute beauty to only one of the two sexes: the

sex, which, however Fair, is always Second. Associating beauty with women has put beauty even further on the defensive, morally.

4 A beautiful woman, we say in English. But a handsome man. "Handsome" is the masculine equivalent of—and refusal of—a compliment which has accumulated certain demeaning overtones, by being reserved for women only. That one can call a man "beautiful" in French and in Italian suggests that Catholic countries—unlike those countries shaped by the Protestant version of Christianity—still retain some vestiges of the non-religious admiration for beauty. But the difference, if one exists, is of degree only. In every modern country that is Christian or post-Christian, women are the beautiful sex—to the harm of the notion of beauty as well as of women.

5 To be called beautiful is thought to name something essential to women's character and concerns. (In contrast to men—whose essence is to be strong, or effective, or competent.) It does not take someone in the throes of advanced feminist awareness to perceive that the way women are taught to be involved with beauty encourages excessive self-admiration or love, and reinforces dependence and immaturity. Everybody (women and men) knows that. For it is "everybody," a whole society, that has identified being feminine with caring about how one looks. (In contrast to being masculine—which is identified with caring about what one is and does and only secondarily, if at all, about how one looks.) Given these stereotypes, it is no wonder that beauty enjoys, at best, a rather mixed reputation.

6 It is not, of course, the desire to be beautiful that is wrong but the obligation to be—or to try. What is accepted by most women as a flattering idealization of their sex is a way of making women feel inferior to what they actually are—or normally grow to be. For the ideal of beauty is administered as a form of self-oppression. Women are taught to see their bodies in parts, and to evaluate each part separately. Breasts, feet, hips, waistline, neck, eyes, nose, complexion, hair, and so on—each in turn is submitted to an anxious, discontented, often despairing inspection.

Even if some pass muster, some will always be found wanting. Nothing less than perfection will do.

7 In men, good look is a whole, something taken in at a glance. It does not need to be confirmed by giving measurements of different regions of the body, nobody encourages a man to dissect his appearance, feature by feature. As for perfection, that is considered trivial—almost unmanly. Indeed, in the ideally good-looking man a small imperfection or blemish is considered positively desirable. According to one movie critic (a woman) who is a declared Robert Redford fan, it is having that cluster of skin-colored moles on one cheek that saves Redford from being merely a "pretty face". Think of the depreciation of women—as well as of beauty—that is implied in that judgment.

8 "The privileges of beauty are immense," said Cocteau. To be sure, beauty is a form of power. And deservedly so. What is lamentable is that it is the only form of power that most women are encouraged to seek. This power is always conceived in the relation to men; it is not the power to do but the power to attract. It is a power that negates itself. For this power is not one that can be chosen freely—at least, not by women—or renounced without social censure.

9 To preen, for a woman, can never be just a pleasure. It is also a duty. It is her work. If a woman does real work—and even if she has clambered up to a leading position in politics, law, medicine, business, or whatever—she is always under pressure to confess that she still works at being attractive. But in so far she is keeping up as one on the Fair Sex she brings under suspicion her very capacity to be objective, professional, authoritative, thoughtful. Damned if they do—women are. And damned if they don't.

10 One could hardly ask for more important evidence of the dangers of considering persons as split between what is "inside" and what is "outside" than that interminable half-comic half-tragic tale, the oppression of women. How easy it is to start off by defining women as

caretakers of their surfaces, and then to degrade them (or find them adorable) for being "superficial." It is a crude trap, and it has worked for too long. But to get out of the trap requires that women get some critical distance from that excellence and privilege which is beauty, enough distance to see how much beauty itself has been abridged in order to prop up the mythology of the "feminine". There should be a way of saving beauty f rom women—and f or them.

(By *Susan Sontag*; Taken from *An American Reader*)

WORDS AND PHRASES

abridge *v.*	restrict one's rights
adrift【ə'drift】*adj.*	floating
arbitrary【a:bitrəri】*adj.*	based on one's own wishes or will
censure【'senʃə】*n.*	rebuke
clamber【'klæmbə】*v.*	climb with difficulty
cluster【'klʌstə】*n.*	a number of
complexion【kəm'plekʃn】*n.*	color of skin
disciple【di'saipl】*n.*	believer in or follower of thought or teaching
enchantment【in'tʃa:ntmənt】*n.*	great delight
Fair(pun)	referring to women
in the throes of	struggling with
interminable【in'tə:minəbl】*adj.*	endless
lamely【'leimli】*adv.*	unconvincingly
mole【məul】*n.*	痣
muster【'mʌstə】*n.*	come up to the required standard
overtone【'əuvətəun】*n.*	a hint or suggestion
paradoxical【ˌpærə'dɔksikəl】*adj.*	self-contradictory
pedagogical【ˌpedə'gɔdʒikl】*adj.*	of science or art of teaching
post-Christian(countries)	dragged behind in believing in Christianity

preen[pri:n] *v.*	dress with elaborate care
prop up	hold up by placing a support
renounce[ri'nauns] *v.*	declare to give up
Second	the second sex(women)
vestige['vestidʒ] *n.*	trace of something gone

I. Understanding the Text

◇ *Understand the subject matter.*

◇ *Read for the main information.*

◇ *Learn the writing technique.*

◇ *Reach the conclusion.*

1. What is the theme of this passage?

____

2. What are the main points made in this passage?

   Para. 1 – 2: ______________________________

   Para. 3 – 4: ______________________________

   Para. 5 – 7: ______________________________

   Para. 8: ______________________________

   Para. 9: ______________________________

3. What is the concluding remark made in this passage?

   Para. 10: ______________________________

II. Analyzing the Paragraphs

◇ *Summarize the information.*

◇ *Generalize the main idea.*

◇ *Find out the topic sentence.*

1. What is the main idea of Paragraph 1?

____

2. What is the main idea of Paragraph 2?

____

3. What is the main idea of Paragraph 3?

____

4. What is the main idea of Paragraph 4?

____

5. What is the main idea of Paragraph 5?

____

6. What is the main idea of Paragraph 6?

____

7. What is the main idea of Paragraph 7?

____

8. What is the main idea of Paragraph 8?

____

9. What is the main idea of Paragraph 9?

____

10. Which is the concluding sentence in Paragraph 10?

____

III. Learning the Language

◇ *Be aware of and sensitive to language variations and varieties.*

◇ *Choose the language as being used in the passage.*

◇ *Learn the best language.*

1. The well-born young Athenians who gathered around Socrates found it quite ________ that their hero was so intelligent, so brave, so honorable, so seductive and so ugly. (Para. 1)

   A) paradoxical　　B) paradox
   C) being paradoxical　　D) to be paradoxical

2. Several thousand years later, we are more cautious ________ the enchantments of beauty. (Para. 2)

   A) with　　B) about　　C) on　　D) in

3. For close to two centuries it has become a convention to ________ beauty to only one of the two sexes. (Para. 3)

   A) tribute　　B) distribute　　C) contribute　　D) attribute

4. That one can call a man "beautiful" in French and in Italian suggests

that Catholic countries—unlike those countries ________ by the Protestant version of Christianity—still retain some vestiges of the non-religious admiration for beauty. (Para. 4)

A) developed B) provided C) shaped D) formed

5. It does not take someone ________ advanced feminist awareness to perceive that the way women are taught to be involved with beauty encourages excessive self-admiration or love. (Para. 5)

A) in the hand of B) in the control of

C) in the eyes of D) in the throes of

6. For it is "everybody", a whole society, that has identified being feminine ________ caring about how one looks. (Para. 5)

A) with B) to C) for D) at

7. Even if some pass muster, some will always be found wanting. ________ less than perfection will do. (Para. 6)

A) Nothing B) Everything C) No thing D) Every thing

8. In men, good look is a whole, something ________ at a glance. (Para. 7)

A) taken with B) taken in C) taken for D) taken out

9. To preen, for a woman, can never be just a pleasure. She is always under pressure to confess that she still works ________ being attractive. (Para. 9)

A) for B) in C) at D) with

10. How easy it is to start off by defining women as caretakers of their surfaces, and then to degrade them for being "superficial". It is a ________ trap, and it has worked for too long. (Para. 10)

A) cruise B) crucial C) cruel D) crude

IV. Thinking Openly

◇ *Keep your mind open to new ideas.*

◇ *Be receptive to other's opinions.*

◇ *Challenge your own judgment.*

1. For the Greeks, beauty was a virtue: a kind of excellence. What does beauty mean to you? (Para. 1)

____

____

2. For close to two centuries it has become a convention to attribute beauty to only one of the two sexes: the second sex. Does it apply to our Chinese convention too? (Para. 3)

____

____

3. A beautiful woman, we say in English. But a handsome man. What are the Chinese words or characters we say to such a man? (Para. 4)

____

____

4. In every modern country that is Christian or post-Christian, women are the beautiful sex. In doing so, harm is done to the notion of beauty as well as of women. Do you agree? (Para. 4)

____

____

5. A woman cares about how she looks, and a man cares about what one is and does and only secondarily, if at all, about how he looks. What do you think? (Para. 5)

____

____

6. It is not, of course, the desire to be beautiful that is wrong, but the obligation to be—or to try. What is the difference between a desire to be beautiful and an obligation to be beautiful? (Para. 6)

____

____

7. Women are taught to see their bodies in parts, and to evaluate each part separately. In men, good look is a whole. What do you think?

(Para. 6 –7)

____

____

8. As for perfection, that is considered trivial—almost unmanly. What is your point of view? (Para. 7)

____

____

V. Thinking Critically

◇ *Be critical in your thinking.*

◇ *Be skeptical in your thinking.*

◇ *Be introspective in your thinking.*

1. Persons then were assumed to be what we now have to call—lamely, enviously—whole persons. Do you have a "whole person" in your mind?

____

____

2. How full paradoxes life really was. What in your mind is the most striking paradox in our social life and in your personal life as well?

____

____

3. Christianity limits excellence (virtue) to moral virtue only. That is to say, Christianity places "moral beauty" above physical charm. What is your preference, moral beauty, physical charm or both? Why?

____

____

4. Associating beauty with women has put beauty even further on the defensive, morally. What is your comment?

____

____

5. Beauty is not the power to do but the power to attract. What is your

understanding of "the power to do and the power to attract"?

____

____

6. It (beauty) is a power that negates itself. In what way does the power of beauty negate itself?

____

____

7. The point(s) that I do not agree with the writer.

____

____

VI. Thinking Independently

◇ *Develop and form ideas or opinions of your own.*

◇ *Be both inductive and deductive in your thinking.*

◇ *Communicate and share with others.*

◇ *Write and present your composition on one of the following topics.*

1. On beauty
2. Beauty in my eyes
3. The privileges of beauty
4. Beauty is no one's privilege
5. The kind of beauty that lasts longer
6. One thing I have learned from this passage

Passage 13

WIN WITH YOUR STRENGTHS

1 Jan Miller, at age 27, was supervising 20 employees at a Mid-western consulting firm. Like many ambitious young people, she thought a position in management was the only route to success. "In the corporate world," Miller says, "people think that if they aren't in management, they haven't arrived. They fall into the trap of ladder climbing."

2 Although Miller had attained a relatively high rung on that ladder, she felt unfulfilled. So she gave up her managerial job and became an analyst within the same company. Her one-on-one work with clients now played to her strengths and gave her a sense of accomplishment. Ten years later, she still feels she made the right decision.

3 Instead of spending time trying to correct your weaknesses—as many of us are taught to do—our experience suggests you should focus on your special talents. For every strength you have, you also possess a multitude of non-strengths. It would be a huge waste of energy to try to fix all your weaknesses. Here are some tips for developing your natural abilities.

4 Being a Renaissance man is in fashion nowadays, yet most people pursuing multiple strengths will achieve only mediocrity in the long run.

5 In 1921 Lewis M. Terman, a Stanford University psychologist, began studying 1440 genius-level children throughout their lifetimes. When

Terman retired, others continued his work. Eventually the data showed that exceptional intelligence doesn't guarantee extraordinary accomplishment. Instead, it seemed clear that what distinguished spectacular achievers from low achievers was that the former were focused on what they wanted to do in life.

6 Clint Black, the Country Music Association's Male Vocalist of the Year in 1990, always knew he was a singer even while holding a job as an ironworker. But he didn't take his future for granted. He knew his voice would improve only if he pursued every opportunity to ply his strength performing in clubs, on porches at church gatherings. His hard work led to a distinct style and created a following.

7 While daily practice is needed to improve the strengths necessary to break into a field, it's also the norm for successful people at their peak. Two-time U. S. Open winner Curtis Strange hits a couple of hundred golf balls a day in addition to his regular physical conditioning.

8 World-class sports figures, musicians and writers have learned that talent alone doesn't guarantee success. Ultimate excellence is a product of total commitment, hard work over the long-term and heeding the message, "If it doesn't feel good, you're not practicing a strength."

9 One of the great mistakes people make is believing they must correct their weaknesses before they can capitalize on their strength. Instead, you should work on a problem only if it's lessening your productivity or self-esteem. By thus "managing" your weaknesses, you allow your strengths to overpower them, ultimately making them irrelevant.

10 In *Vince*, the biography of Vince Lombardi, author Michael O'Brien notes that the legendary coach of the Green Bay Packers football team recognized the importance of not allowing his players to focus on their weaknesses. Before a game with the Detroit lions, Lombardi showed films of only the successful running plays previously used against the Lions. That way, his team would be more likely to take the field with confidence.

11 Look at logic. When are you most confident? Recalling a moment of success or a moment of failure? Individuals are always stronger when they have their successes clearly in mind.

12 Some strengths reveal themselves only when combined with those of other people. In his autobiography, Jerry Lewis recalls that as a young comedian performing in small clubs, he enjoyed only moderate success with his slapstick. One day, after a club singer had bombed, Lewis recommended a friend named Dean Martin as a replacement. Because Lewis had already told the club owner that he and Martin did a comedy routine together, the two were forced to come up with an act. Within days, the duo was performing in Atlantic City before enthusiastic crowds. By 1949, their first movie together, *My Friend Irma*, was a box-office smash, and Dean Martin and Jerry Lewis went on to become one of the most successful comedy teams in film history.

13 Stephen J. Cannell is a prolific television writer and producer. Since his studio was founded in 1980, it has produced over two dozen prime-time series, including *The A-Team*, *Wiseguy*, *Hunter* and *The Commish.* Writing is Connell's strength. Unfortunately, his weakness is dyslexia, a condition that causes him to transpose numbers and letters.

14 "I'm bad at spelling and sequencing," he explains, "all the things that gave me trouble in high school." Yet instead of expending energy trying to correct a lifelong problem, Cannell types his scripts and then has an assistant smooth out the rough spots.

15 Everyone needs support of some sort. It can be as simple as eyeglasses to correct poor vision. Or, as in the case of one CEO who is an accident-prone driver, it might be the help of a college student to provide transportation to meetings.

16 Do we mean you shouldn't even try to work on problem areas? Of course not. But at some point you'll have to decide whether your efforts are fruitful. If the answer is no, then stop and apply the same energy to what you're good at.

17 When Delores Calcagno was vice president of training for Prudential Securities, she applied this thinking to Prudential's hiring and management practices. "We focused on the individual and his or her strengths," Calcagno says. "We didn't ask guys who liked to make cold-calls to service existing accounts, or women who liked trading options to sell annuities." Calcagno, now with Prudential Mutual Fund Management, is emphatic on this point. "If you don't focus on strengths," she says, "you're playing a losing game."

Words and Phrases

annuity【əˈnjuːəti】*n.*	annual income
attain【əˈtein】*v.*	accomplish something
duo【ˈdjuːəu】*n.*	two performers singing or playing together
dyslexia【disˈleksiə】*n.*	inability to read
emphatic【imˈfætik】*adj.*	of emphasis
heed【hiːd】*v.*	pay serious attention to
norm【nɔːm】*n.*	standard; model
ply【plai】*v.*	use diligently as a tool/weapon
prolific【prəˈlifik】*adj.*	productive
prone【prəun】*adj.*	be subject to
prudential【pruˈdenʃəl】*adj.*	exercising good judgment or common sense
Renaissance【riˈneisəns】	文艺复兴
rung【rʌŋ】*n.*	a bar forming a step of a ladder
slapstick【ˈslæpstik】*n.*	a paddle designed to produce a loud sound
smash【smæʃ】*n.*	a hit; a success
spectacular【spekˈtækjulə】*adj.*	very grand
transpose【trænsˈpəuz】*v.*	reverse the order or place of

I. Understanding the Text

◇ *Understand the subject matter.*

◇ *Read for the main information.*

◇ *Learn the writing technique.*

◇ *Reach the conclusion.*

1. What is the theme of this passage?

____

2. What are the main points made in the passage?

   Para. 1 – 2: ______________________________________

   Para. 3 – 16: _____________________________________

3. What is the conclusion drawn in this passage?

   Para. 17: ____

II. Analyzing the Paragraphs

◇ *Summarize the information.*

◇ *Generalize the main idea.*

◇ *Find out the topic sentence.*

1. What is the main idea of Paragraph 1 and 2?

____

2. What is the main idea of Paragraph 3?

____

3. What are the tips for developing your natural abilities?

   Para. 4 – 5: ______________________________________

   Para. 6 – 8: ______________________________________

   Para. 9 – 11: _____________________________________

   Para. 12: ____

   Para. 13 – 16: ____________________________________

4. What is the main idea of Paragraph 17?

____

III. Learning the Language

◇ *Be aware of and sensitive to language variations and varieties.*

◇ *Choose the language as being used in the passage.*

◇ *Learn the best language.*

1. Jan Miller, at age 27, was ________ 20 employees at a Mid-western consulting firm. (Para. 1)

   A) supervising　　B) managing　　C) controlling　　D) handling

2. Her ________ work with clients now played to her strengths and gave her a sense of accomplishment. (Para. 2)

   A) one-by-one　　B) one-on-one

   C) one-to-one　　D) one-and-one

3. It would be a huge waste of energy to try to ________ all your weaknesses. (Para. 3)

   A) repair　　B) revise　　C) fix　　D) mend

4. Being a Renaissance man is in fashion nowadays, yet most people pursuing multiple strengths will achieve only mediocrity ________. (Para. 4)

   A) in a long way　　B) in the long way

   C) in a long run　　D) in the long run

5. Ultimate excellence is a product of total commitment, hard work over the long-term and ________ the message, "If it doesn't feel good, you're not practicing a strength." (Para. 8)

   A) heal　　B) heeling　　C) heed　　D) heeding

6. One of the great mistakes people make is believing they must correct their weaknesses before they can ________ their strength. (Para. 9)

   A) capitalize on　　B) invest in

   C) profit from　　D) take advantage of

7. Before a game with the Detroit lions, Lombardi showed films of only the successful running plays previously used against the Lions. That way, his team would be more likely to ________ the field with confidence. (Para. 10)

A) get　B) take　C) occupy　D) seize

8. Stephen J. Cannell is a ________ television writer and producer. Since his studio was founded in 1980, it has produced over dozen prime-time series. (Para. 13)

A) emphatic　B) prudent　C) profile　D) prolific

9. Everyone needs support of some sort. It can be as simple as eyeglasses to ________ poor vision. (Para. 15)

A) adjust　B) improve　C) correct　D) right

10. Calcagno, now with Prudential Mutual Fund Management, is ________ on this point. "If you don't focus on strengths," she says, "you're playing a losing game." (Para. 17)

A) pathetic　B) sympathetic　C) phatic　D) emphatic

IV. Thinking Openly

◇ *Keep your mind open to new ideas.*

◇ *Be receptive to other's opinions.*

◇ *Challenge your own judgment.*

1. Instead of spending time trying to correct your weaknesses—as many of us are taught to do—our experience suggests you should focus on your special talents. What's your opinion? (Para. 3)

____

____

2. For every strength you have, you also possess a multitude of non-strengths. Do you agree? What are your strengths and non-strengths then? (Para. 3)

____

____

3. It would be a huge waste of energy to try to fix all your weaknesses. What do you think? (Para. 3)

____

____

4. Yet most people pursuing multiple strengths will achieve only mediocrity in the long run. Do you think the same way? (Para. 4)

____

____

5. What distinguishes spectacular achievers from low achievers is that the former are focused on what they want to do in life. Do you agree? What is your focus in life? (Para. 5)

____

____

6. Individuals are always stronger when they have their successes clearly in mind. What are your successes? Do you often keep them in your mind? (Para. 11)

____

____

7. Some strengths reveal themselves only when combined with those of other people. What can your learn from this statement? (Para. 12)

____

____

V. Thinking Critically

◇ *Be critical in your thinking.*

◇ *Be skeptical in your thinking.*

◇ *Be introspective in your thinking.*

1. What is your viewpoint on the theme of this passage "Win with Your Strengths."?

____

____

2. People think that if they aren't in management, they haven't arrived. What do you think?

____

____

3. What is fulfillment? What do you do to make you feel fulfilled?

____

____

4. The data showed that exceptional intelligence doesn't guarantee extraordinary accomplishment. What do you think can better guarantee accomplishment?

____

____

5. While daily practice is needed to improve the strengths necessary to break into a field, it's also the norm for successful people at their peak. What can you learn from this statement?

____

____

6. Ultimate excellence is a product of total commitment, hard work over the long-term. What do you think?

____

____

7. One of the great mistakes people make is believing they must correct their weaknesses before they can capitalize on their strength. What is the appropriate way to manage one's weaknesses?

____

____

8. Everyone needs support of some sort. It can be as simple as eyeglasses to correct poor vision. What is your weakness that needs to be corrected?

____

____

9. The point(s) that I do not agree with the writer.

____

____

VI. Thinking Independently

◇ *Develop and form ideas or opinions of your own.*

◇ *Be both inductive and deductive in your thinking.*

◇ *Communicate and share with others.*

◇ *Write and present your composition on one of the following topics.*

1. On failure
2. My strengths and weaknesses
3. My view on perfection
4. My way to success
5. A man can be destroyed but can not be defeated.
6. I can accept failure, but can not accept not trying.
7. One thing I have learned from this passage

Passage 14

THE WORKER AS CREATOR OR MACHINE

1 Unless man exploits, he has to work in order to live. However primitive and simple his method of work may be, by the very fact of production, he has risen above the animal kingdom; rightly has he been defined as "the animal that produces." But work is not only an inescapable necessity for man. Work is also his liberator from nature, his creator as a social and independent being. In the process of work, that is, the molding and changing of nature outside of himself, man molds and changes himself. He emerges from nature by mastering her, he develops his powers of co-operation, of reason, his sense of beauty. He separates himself from nature, from the original unity with her, but at the same time unites himself with her again as her master and builder. The more his work develops, the more his individuality develops. In molding nature and re-creating her, he learns to make use of his powers, increasing his skill and creativeness.

2 In Western history, craftsmanship, especially as it developed in the thirteenth and fourteenth centuries, constitutes one of the peaks in the evolution of creative work. Work was not a useful activity, but one which carried with it a profound satisfaction. The main features of craftsmanship

have been very clearly expressed by C. W. Mills[1]. "There is no ulterior motive in work other than the product being made and the processes of its creation. The details of daily work are meaningful because they are not detached in the worker's mind from the product of the work. The worker is free to control his own working action. The craftsman is thus able to learn from his work; and to use and develop his capacities and skills in its prosecution. There is no split of work and play, or work and culture. The craftsman's way of livelihood determines and infuses his entire mode of living."

3 With the collapse of the medieval structure, and the beginning of the modern mode of production, the meaning and function of work changed fundamentally, especially in the Protestant countries[2]. Man, being afraid of his newly won freedom, was obsessed by the need to subdue his doubts and fears by developing a feverish activity. The outcome of this activity, success or failure, decided his salvation, indicating whether he was among the saved or the lost souls. Work, instead of being an activity satisfying in itself and pleasurable, became a duty and an obsession. The more it was possible to gain riches by work, the more it became a pure means to the aim of wealth and success.

4 However, work in this sense existed only for the upper and middle classes, those who could amass some capital and employ the work of others. For the vast majority of those who had only their physical energy to sell, work became nothing but forced labor. The first centuries of the modern era find the meaning of work divided into that of duty among the middle class, and that of forced labor among those without property.

5 What happens to the industrial worker? He spends his best energy for seven or eight hours a day in producing "something." He needs his work in order to make a living, but his role is essentially a passive one. He fulfills a small isolated function in a complicated and highly organized process of production, and is never confronted with "his" product as a whole, at least not as a producer, but only as a consumer, provided he has the money to buy "his" product in a store. He is put in a certain

place, has to carry out a certain task, but does not participate in the organization or management of the work. The shoes, the cars, the electric bulbs, are produced by "the enterprise", using the machines. He is a part of the machine, rather than its master as an active agent. The machine, instead of being in his service to do work for him, has become his master. Instead of the machine being the substitute for human energy, man has become a substitute for the machine. His work can be defined as the performance of acts which cannot yet be performed by machines.

6 Work is a means of getting money, not in itself a meaningful human activity. P. Drucker, observing workers in the automobile industry, expresses this idea very succinctly: "For the great majority of automobile workers, the only meaning of the job is in the pay check, not in anything connected with the work or the product. Work appears as something unnatural, a disagreeable, meaningless condition of getting the pay check, devoid of dignity as well as of importance. No wonder that this puts a premium on slovenly work, on slowdowns, and on other tricks to get the same pay check with less work. No wonder that this results in an unhappy and discontented worker—because a pay check is not enough to base one's self-respect on."

7 This relationship of the worker to his work is an outcome of the whole social organization of which he is a part. Being "employed", he is not an active agent, has no responsibility except the proper performance of the isolated piece of work he is doing, and has little interest except the one of bringing home enough money to support himself and his family. Nothing more is expected of him, or wanted from him. He is part of the equipment hired by capital, and his role and function are determined by this quality of being a piece of equipment. In recent decades, increasing attention has been paid to the psychology of the worker, and to his attitude toward his work, to "the human problem of industry"; but this very formulation is indicative of the underlying attitude; there is a human being spending most of his lifetime at work, and what should be discussed is "the industrial

problem of human beings", rather than "the human problem of industry".

8 Most investigations in the field of industrial psychology are concerned with the question of how the productivity of the individual worker can be increased, and how he can be made to work with less friction; psychology has lent its services to "human engineering", an attempt to treat the worker and employee like a machine which runs better when it is well oiled. The underlying idea can be formulated like this: if he works better when he is happy, then let us make him happy, secure, satisfied, or anything else, provided it raises his output and diminishes friction.

9 The alienated and profoundly unsatisfactory character of work results in two reactions: one, the ideal of complete laziness; the other a deep-seated, though often unconscious hostility toward work.

10 It is not difficult to recognize the widespread longing for the state of complete laziness and passivity. There are, of course, many useful and labor saving gadgets. But this usefulness often serves only as a rationalization for the appeal to complete passivity and receptivity.

11 But there is far more serious and deep-seated reaction to the meaninglessness and boredom of work. It is hostility toward work which is much less conscious than our craving for laziness and inactivity. Many a businessman has a feeling of fraudulency about his product and a secret contempt for it. He hates his customers, who force him to put up a show in order to sell. He hates his competitors because they are a threat; his employees as well as his superiors, because he is in a constant competitive fight with them. Most important of all, he hates himself, because he sees his life passing by, without making any sense beyond the momentary intoxication of success. Of course, this hate and contempt for others and for oneself, and for the very things one produces, is mainly unconscious, and only occasionally comes up to awareness in a fleeting thought, which is sufficiently disturbing to be set aside as quickly as possible.

(Adapted from *A Rhetorical Reader*, *Invention and Design*)

Notes on the Text

[1] C. W. Mills: author of White Collar (1951), from which this quotation is taken.

[2] the Protestant countries: referring to Germany, Switzerland, Scandinavia, the Netherlands, the British Isles and early America.

WORDS AND PHRASES

amass *v.*	accumulate, collect
bliss【blis】*n.*	great happiness; perfect joy
devoid *adj.*	empty of; lacking in something
formulation【ˌfɔːmjuˈleiʃn】*n.*	the way of defining a problem
fraudulency【ˈfrɔːdjulənsi】*n.*	deception
gadget【ˈgædʒit】*n.*	a small device
infuse【ˈinfjuːs】*v.*	introduce something into somebody's mind
obsess【əbˈses】*v.*	preoccupy
premium【ˈpriːmjəm】*n.*	prize or reward
prosecution *n.*	the act of carrying out an activity or occupation
rationalization【ˌræʃənəliˈzeiʃən】*n.*	the process of rationalizing something
slovenly【slʌvənli】*adj.*	careless about one's personal hygiene and tidiness
subdue【səbˈdjuː】*v.*	overcome, conquer
succinctly【səkˈsiŋktli】*adv.*	concisely
ulterior【ʌlˈtiəriə】*n.*	lying outside

I. Understanding the Text

◇ *Understand the subject matter.*

◇ *Read for the main information.*

◇ *Learn the writing technique.*

◇ *Reach the conclusion.*

1. What is the theme of this passage?

____

2. What are the main points made in this passage?

Para. 1: ______________________________

Para. 2: ______________________________

Para. 3 – 4: ______________________________

Para. 5 – 8: ______________________________

3. What is the conclusion drawn by the writer?

Para. 9 – 11: ______________________________

II. Analyzing the Paragraphs

◇ *Summarize the information.*

◇ *Generalize the main idea.*

◇ *Find out the topic sentence.*

1. What is the main idea of Paragraph 1?

____

2. What is the main idea of Paragraph 2?

____

3. What is the main idea of Paragraph 3?

____

4. What is the main idea of Paragraph 4?

____

5. What is the main idea of Paragraph 5?

____

6. What is the main idea of Paragraph 6?

____

7. What is the main idea of Paragraph 7?

____

8. What is the main idea of Paragraph 8?

____

9. What is the main idea of Paragraph 9?

____

10. What is the main idea of Paragraph 10?

____

11. What is the main idea of Paragraph 11?

____

III. Learning the Language

◇ *Be aware of and sensitive to language variations and varieties.*

◇ *Choose the language as being used in the passage.*

◇ *Learn the best language.*

1. ________ man exploits, he has to work in order to live. (Para. 1)
   A) Unless B) Provided C) Except D) Except for
2. However primitive and simple his method of work may be, by the very fact of production, he has ________ above the animal kingdom. (Para. 1)
   A) been rising B) risen
   C) been raised D) raised
3. There is no split of work and play, or work and culture. The craftsman' s way of livelihood determines and ________ his entire mode of living." (Para. 2)
   A) fuses B) defuses C) infuses D) profuses
4. With the ________ of the medieval structure, and the beginning of the modern mode of production, the meaning and function of work changed fundamentally. (Para. 3)
   A) end B) ruin C) fall D) collapse
5. Man, being afraid of his newly won freedom, was ________ by the need to subdue his doubts and fears by developing a feverish activity. (Para. 3)
   A) obsessed B) obese C) obscene D) possessed
6. For the vast majority of those who had only their physical energy to

sell, work became nothing ________ forced labor. (Para. 4)

A) except B) but C) besides D) of

7. What happens to the industrial worker? He ________ his best energy for seven or eight hours a day in producing "something." (Para. 5)

A) burns B) expends C) spends D) devotes

8. Work appears as something unnatural, a disagreeable, meaningless condition of getting the pay check, ________ dignity as well as of importance. (Para. 6)

A) void of B) involving C) avoiding D) devoid of

9. In recent decades, increasing attention has been paid to the psychology of the worker, and to the "human problem of industry"; but this very formulation is ________ the underlying attitude; what should be discussed is the "industrial problem of human being," rather than "the human problem of industry." (Para. 7)

A) indicating B) to indicate

C) to indicating D) indicative of

10. It is a hostility toward work which is much less conscious than our ________ laziness and inactivity. (Para. 11)

A) craving for B) caring for

C) begging for D) requiring for

IV. Thinking Openly

◇ *Keep your mind open to new ideas.*

◇ *Be receptive to other's opinions.*

◇ *Challenge your own judgment.*

1. But work is not only an inescapable necessity for man. What do you think are the other necessities for man? (Para. 1)

____

____

2. In the process of work, that is, the molding and changing of nature outside of himself, man molds and changes himself. What do you

think? (Para. 1)

____

____

3. The more his work develops, the more his individuality develops. Do you agree? (Para. 1)

____

____

4. Instead of the machine being the substitute for human energy, man has become a substitute for the machine. What do you think of this analysis? (Para. 5)

____

____

5. Work is a means of getting money, not in itself a meaningful human activity. Do you think that work itself is a meaningful activity? (Para. 6)

____

____

6. If he works better when he is happy, then let us make him happy, secure, satisfied, or anything else, provided it raises his output and diminishes friction. What's your comment on this? (Para. 8)

____

____

7. People tend to long for the state of complete laziness and passivity. Do you think of that as part of human nature? (Para. 10)

____

____

V. Thinking Critically

◇ *Be critical in your thinking.*

◇ *Be skeptical in your thinking.*

◇ *Be introspective in your thinking.*

1. The more it was possible to gain riches by work, the more it became a pure means to the aim of wealth and success. What do you think?

____

____

2. A pay check is not enough to base one's self-respect on. What else are needed to base one's self-respect?

____

____

3. There is a human being spending most of his lifetime at work, and what should be discussed is "the industrial problem of human beings", rather than "the human problem of industry". Which indeed is the issue to be discussed: "the industrial problem of human beings" or "the human problem of industry"?

____

____

5. The point(s) that I do not agree with the writer.

____

____

VI. Thinking Independently

◇ *Develop and form ideas or opinions of your own.*

◇ *Be both inductive and deductive in your thinking.*

◇ *Communicate and share with others.*

◇ *Write and present your composition on one of the following topics.*

1. What does work mean to me?
2. Work and play
3. What do I expect from work?
4. In the process of work, man molds and changes himself.
5. Pay-check is not enough to base one's self-respect on.
6. Laziness and passivity
7. One thing I have learned from this passage

Passage 15

LOVE IS A FALLACY

[**of the characters**]

THE NARRATOR: Cool was I and logical. Keen, calculating, perspicacious, acute—I was all of these. My brain was as powerful as a dynamo, as precise as a chemist's scales, as penetrating as a scalpel. And—think of it! —I was only eighteen. I was now thinking of having Petey's girl friend, Polly.

PETEY BURCH: It isn't often that one so young has such a giant intellect. Take, for example, Petey Burch, my roommate at the University of Minnesota. Same age, same background, but dumb as an ox. A nice enough young fellow, you understand, but nothing upstairs. Emotional type. Unstable. Impressionable. Worst of all, a faddist. Fads, I submit, are the very negation of reason. To be swept up in every new craze that comes along, to surrender yourself to idiocy just because everybody else is doing it—this, to me, is the greatest of mindlessness. His girl friend is Polly Espy. But what he needs badly now is a raccoon to follow the fad.

POLLY ESPY: A beautiful and yet seemingly dull girl in the same university, who is now dating Petey.

[**The narrator is reading out his mind**]

1 I was a freshman in law school. In a few years I would be out in

practice. I was well aware of the importance of the right kind of wife in furthering a lawyer's career. The successful lawyers I had observed were, almost without exceptions, married to beautiful, gracious, intelligent women. With one omission, Polly fitted these specifications perfectly.

2 Beautiful she was. She was not yet of pin-up proportions, but I felt sure the time would supply the lack. She already had the makings.

3 Gracious she was. By gracious I mean full of graces. She had an erectness of carriage, an ease of bearing, a poise that clearly indicated the best of breeding. At table her manners were exquisite.

4 Intelligent she was not. In fact, she went in the opposite direction. But I believed that under my guidance she would smarten up. At any rate, it was worth a try. It is, after all, easier to make a beautiful dumb girl smart than to make an ugly smart girl beautiful.

[**A talk between the two men**]

5 "Petey," I said, "are you in love with Polly Espy?"

6 "I think she's a keen kid," he replied, "but I don't know if you'd call it love. Why?"

7 "Do you," I asked, "have any kind of formal arrangement with her? I mean are you going steady or anything like that?"

8 "No. We see each other quite a bit, but we both have other dates. Why?"

9 "Is there," I asked, "any other man for whom she has a particular fondness?"

10 "Not that I know of. Why?"

11 I nodded with satisfaction. "In other words, if you were out of the picture, the field would be open. Is that right?"

12 "I guess so. What are you getting at?"

13 "Nothing, nothing," I said innocently, and took a raccoon out of my suitcase from the closet. "Would you like it?" I asked.

14 "Oh yes!" he cried, snatching the fur coat from me. Then a cautious

look came into his eyes. "What do you want for it?"

15 "Your girl," I said, directly and forcefully.

16 "Polly?" he said in a horrified whisper. "You want Polly?"

17 "That's right."

18 He flung the coat from him. "Never," he said sternly.

19 I shrugged. "Okay. If you don't want to be in the swim, I guess it's your business."

20 I sat down in a chair and pretended to read a book, but out of the corner of my eye I kept watching Petey. He was a torn man. First he looked at the coat with the expression of a hungry homeless child at a bakery window. Then he turned away and set his jaw resolutely. Then he looked back at the coat, with even more longing in his face. Then he turned away, but without so much resolution this time. Back and forth his head turned, desire for it grew stronger.

21 "It isn't as though I was in love with Polly," he said thickly. "or going steady or anything like that."

22 "That's right," I murmured.

23 "Try on the coat," said I.

24 He acted accordingly. "Fits fine," he said happily.

25 I rose from my chair. "Is it a deal?" I asked, extending my hand.

26 He swallowed. "It's a deal," he said and shook my hand.

[**The first date**]

27 I had my first date with Polly the following evening. This was in nature of a survey; I want to find out just how much work I had to do to get her mind to the standard I required.

28 I went back to my room with a heavy heart. I had gravely underestimated the size of my task. This girl's lack of information was terrifying. Nor would it be enough merely to support her with information. First she had to be taught to think. At first I was tempted to give her back to Petey. But then I got to think about her abundant physical charms and

about the way she entered a room and the way she handled a knife and fork, and I decided to make an effort.

[**The first class on logic**]

29 I went about it, as in all things, systematically. I gave her a course in logic. It happened that I, as a law student, was taking a course in logic myself, so I had all the facts at my finger tips. "Polly," I said to her when I picked her up on our next date, "tonight we are going to talk about logic."

30 She thought this over for a minute and decided she liked it. "Magnificent," she said.

31 "Logic," I said, clearing my throat, "is the science of thinking. Before we can think correctly, we must first learn to recognize the common fallacies of logic. These we will take up tonight."

32 "Wow-dow!" she cried, clapping her hands delightedly.

33 I went bravely on. "First let us examine the fallacy called Dicto Simpliciter."

34 "By all means," she urged, batting her lashes eagerly.

35 "Dicto Simpliciter means an argument based on an unqualified generalization. For example: Exercise is good. Therefore everybody should exercise."

36 "I agree," said Polly earnestly. "I mean exercise is wonderful. I mean it builds the body and everything."

37 "Polly," I said gently, "the argument is a fallacy. Exercise is good is an unqualified generalization. For instance, if you have heart disease, exercise is bad, not good. Many people are ordered by their doctors not to exercise. You must qualify the generalization. You must say exercise is usually good, or exercise is good for most people. Otherwise, you committed a Dicto Simpliciter. Do you see?"

38 "No," she confessed. "But this is marvy. Do more! Do more!"

39 "It will be better if you stop pulling at my sleeve," I told her, and

when she stopped, I continued. "Next we take up a fallacy called Hasty Generalization. Listen carefully: You can't speak French. I can't speak French. Petey Burch can't speak French. I must therefore conclude that nobody at the University of Minnesota can speak French."

40 "Really?" said Polly, amazed. "Nobody?"

41 I hid my irritation. "Polly, it's a fallacy. The generalization is reached too hastily. There are too few instances to support such a conclusion."

42 "Know any more fallacies?" she asked breathlessly. "This is more fun than dancing even."

43 I fought off a wave of despair. I was getting nowhere with this girl, absolutely nowhere. Still, I am nothing if not persistent.

44 "Next comes Post Hoc. Listen to this: Let's not take Bill on our picnic. Every time we take him out with us, it rains."

45 "I know somebody like that," she exclaimed. "A girl back home—Eula Becker, her name is. It never fails. Every single time we take her on a picnic…."

46 "Polly," I said sharply, "it's a fallacy. Eula Becker doesn't cause the rain. She has no connection with the rain. You are guilt of Post Hoc if you blame Eula Becker."

47 "I'll never do that again," she promised. "Are you mad at me?"

48 I sighed deeply. "No, Polly, I'm not mad."

49 I consulted my watch. "I think we'd better call it a night. I'll take you home now."

50 I deposited her at the girl's dormitory, where she assured me that she had a perfectly terrify evening, and I went gloomily to my room. Petey lay snoring in his bed. For a moment I considered waking him and telling him that he could have his girl back. It seemed clear that my project was doomed to failure. The girl simply had a logic-proof head.

51 But then I reconsidered. I had wasted one evening: I might as well waste another. Who knew? I decided to give it one more try.

[**The second class**]

52 Seated under the oak the next evening I said, "Our first fallacy tonight is called Ad Misericordiam."

53 She quivered with delight.

54 "Listen closely," I said. "A man applies for a job. When the boss asks him what his qualifications are, he replies that he has a wife and six children at home, the wife is a helpless cripple, the children have nothing to eat, no clothes to wear, no shoes on their feet, there are no beds in the house, and winter is coming."

55 A tear rolled down each of Polly's pink cheeks. "Oh, this is awful, awful," she sobbed.

56 "Yes, it's awful," I agreed, 'But it's no argument. The man never answered the boss's questions about his qualifications. Instead he appealed to the boss's sympathy. He committed the fallacy of Ad Misericordiam. Do you understand?"

57 "Have you got a handkerchief?" she cried loudly.

58 I handed her a handkerchief and tried to keep from screaming while she wiped her eyes. "Next," I said in a carefully controlled tone, "we will discuss False Analogy. Here is an example: Students should be allowed to look at their textbooks during examinations. After all, surgeons have X-rays to guide them during an operation, lawyers have briefs to guide them during a trial, carpenters have blueprints to guide them when they are building a house. Why, then, shouldn't students be allowed to look at their textbooks during an examination?"

59 "There now," she said enthusiastically, "is the most marvy idea I've heard in years."

60 "Polly," I said angrily, "the argument is all wrong. Doctors, layers, and carpenters aren't taking a test to see how much they have learned, but students are. The situations are altogether different, and you can't make an analogy between them."

61 "I still think it's a good idea," said Polly.

62 "No," I said, almost losing my patience, but continued. "Next we'll try Hypothesis Contrary to Fact."

63 "Sounds yummy(fine)," was Polly's reaction.

64 "Listen: If Madame Curie had not happened to leave a photographic plate in a drawer with a chunk of pitchblende, the world today would not know about radium."

65 "True, true," said Polly, nodding her head.

66 "But I would like to point out that the statement is a fallacy. Maybe Madame Curie could have discovered radium at some later date. Maybe somebody else would have discovered it. Maybe a number of things would have happened. You can't start with a hypothesis that is not true and then draw any supportable conclusions from it."

67 "Maybe, as you said." she said mindlessly.

68 One more chance, I decided. But just one more. There is a limit to what flesh and blood can bear. "The next fallacy is called Poisoning the Well."

69 "How cute!" she gurgled.

70 "Two men are having a debate. The first one gets up and says, 'My opponent is a notorious liar. 'You can't believe a word that he is going to say.' ... Now, Polly, think. Think hard. What's wrong?'

71 I watched her closely as she drew the brows together. Suddenly, a glimmer of intelligence—the first I had seen—came into her eyes. "It's not fair," she said with indignation. "It's not a bit fair. What chance has the second man got if the first man calls him a liar before he even begins talking?"

72 "Right!" I cried. "One hundred percent right. It's not fair. The first man has poisoned the well before anybody could drink from it. Polly, I'm proud of you."

73 "Pshaw," she murmured, blushing with pleasure.

74 "You see, my dear, these things aren't so hard. All you have to do is to concentrate. Think—examine—evaluate."

75 Five nights this took, but it was worth it. I had made a logician out of

Polly; I had taught her to think. My job was done. She was worthy of me at last. She was a fit wife for me, a proper hostess for my many mansions, a suitable mother for my well-off children. It must not be thought that I was without love for this girl. Quite the contrary. I determined to acquaint her with my feeling at our very next meeting. The time had come to change our relationship from academic to romantic.

[**The last date**]

76 "Polly." I said when next we sat beneath our oak, "tonight we will not discuss fallacies."

77 "Aw, gee," she said, disappointed.

78 "My dear," I said, favoring her with a smile, "we have spent five evenings together. We have gotten along splendid. It is clear that we are well matched."

79 "Hasty Generalization," said Polly brightly.

80 "I beg your pardon," said I.

81 "Hasty Generalization," she repeated. "How can you say that we are well matched on the basis of only five dates?"

82 I chuckled with amusement. The dear child had learned her lesson well. "My dear," I said, patting her hand in a tolerant manner, "five dates is plenty. After all, you don't have to eat a whole cake to know it's good."

83 "False Analogy," said Polly promptly. "I'm not a cake. I'm a girl."

84 I chuckled with somewhat less amusement. The dear child had learned her lessons perhaps too well. I decided to change tactics. Obviously the best approach was a smile, direct declaration of love. I paused for a moment while my massive brain chose proper words. Then I began:

85 "Polly, I love you. You are the whole world to me, and the moon and the stars and the constellations of outer space. Please, my darling, say that you will go steady with me, for if you will not, life will be

meaningless. I will languish. I will refuse my meals. I will wander the face of the earth, a shambling, hollow-eyed wreck."

86 There, I thought, folding my arms, that ought to do it.

87 "Ad Misericordiam," said Polly.

88 I ground my teeth as if my monster had me by the throat. At all costs I had to keep cool.

89 "Well, Polly," I said, forcing s smile, "you certainly have learned your fallacies."

90 "You're damn right," she said with a vigorous nod.

91 "And who taught them to you, Polly."

92 "You did."

93 "That's right. So you do owe me something, don't you, my dear? If I hadn't come along you never would have learned about fallacies."

94 "Hypothesis Contrary to Fact," she said instantly.

95 I dashed perspiration from my brow. "Polly," I croaked, "you mustn't take all these things so literally. I mean this is just classroom stuff. You know that the things you learn in school don't have anything to do with life."

96 "Docto Simpliciter," she said, wagging her finger at me playfully.

97 That was the final straw. I leaped to my feet, roaring like a bull. "Will you or will you not go steady with me?"

98 "I will not," she replied.

99 "Why not?" I demanded.

100 "Because this afternoon I promised Petey Burch that I would go steady with him."

101 I staggered back, overcome by the great dishonor of him. After he promised, after he made a dcal, after he shook my hand! "The rat!" I shrieked, kicking up big pieces of grassy earth. "You can't go with him, Polly. He's a liar. He's a cheat. He's a rat."

102 "Poisoning the Well," said Polly, "and stop shouting. I think shouting must be a fallacy too."

103 With an immense effort of will, I changed my voice. "All right," I said. "You're a logician. Let's look at this thing logically. How could you choose Petey Burch over me? Look at me—a brilliant student, a tremendous intellectual, a man with an assured future. Look at Petey—a knot-head, an emotionally unstable person, a guy who'll never know where his next meal is coming from. Can you give me one logical reason why you should go steady with Petey Burch?"

104 "I certainly can," declared Polly. "He's got a raccoon coat."

(By *James Bell* and *Adrian Cohn*; Adapted from *Rhetoric in a Modern Mode*)

WORDS AND PHRASES

acute【əˈkjut】*adj.*	perceptive and intelligent
analogy【əˈnælədʒi】*n.*	the reasoning or explanation given by comparing similar points
bearing *n.*	way of moving or standing
blush *v.*	become red in face
breeding *n.*	upbringing, education and training in one's manners
brow *n.*	forehead
carriage *n.*	way of holding the body
chuckle *v.*	laugh quietly
clap *v.*	applaud
confess *v.*	admit openly a wrongdoing
constellation【kɔnstəˈleiʃən】*n.*	a group of stars
croak【krəuk】*v.*	sound of a frog or crow
dynamo【ˈdainəmou】*n.*	generator of electricity
exquisite【ˈekskwizit】*adj.*	delicate; very fine
fad【fæd】*n.*	a fashion that lasts for a short time
gurgle *v.*	make a bubbling sound of water
idiocy【ˈidiəsi】*n.*	great foolishness; of an idiot
in the swim	familiar with the current tendencies

indignation *n.*	anger mixed with scorn
languish *v.*	be neglected or deprived
lash【læʃ】*n.*	an eyelash
perspicacious【pə:spiˈkeiʃəs】*adj.*	far-seeing; having good judgment
photographic *adj.*	of photography
pin-up *n.*	a picture pinned on a wall
pitchblende【ˈpitʃblend】*n.*	沥青铀
poise *n.*	calm self-assured dignity
pshaw【ʃɔ:】*n.*	expressing disbelief, impatience, or contempt
raccoon【ræku:n】*n.*	浣熊大衣
scalpel【ˈskælpəl】*n.*	a surgeon's sharp knife used in operations
shambling【ˈʃæmbliŋ】*n.*	walking in a lazy or clumsy manner
shriek【ʃri:k】*v.*	give a sharp cry
shrug *n.*	gesture of raising or dropping the shoulders
stagger *v.*	move unsteadily, nearly falling
upstairs(AmE slang)	empty minded
wag *v.*	move something to and fro

I. Understanding the Text

◇ *Understand the subject matter.*

◇ *Read for the main information.*

◇ *Learn the writing technique.*

◇ *Reach the conclusion.*

1. What is the type of writing of this passage?

____

2. What is the CONTEXT of this narration?

____

3. What are the SELECTION OF DETAILS of this narration?

   Para. 1 – 4: ______________________________________

Para. 5 – 26: ______

Para. 27 – 28: ______

Para. 29 – 51: ______

Para. 52 – 75: ______

Para. 76 – 104: ______

4. What is the POINT OF VIEW of this narration?

______

5. What is the ending of this love story?

______

6. What is the PURPOSE of this narration?

______

II. Analyzing the Paragraphs

◇ *Summarize the information.*

◇ *Generalize the main idea.*

◇ *Find out the topic sentence.*

1. How many characters are there in this narration? And who are they?

______

2. What is in the narrator's mind?

   Para. 1 – 4: ______

3. What is the narrator's intention of initiating this talk with Petey Burch?

   Para. 5 – 26: ______

4. What is the first date in nature?

   Para. 27 – 28: ______

5. What fallacies are taught in the first class on logic?

   Para. 29 – 51: ______

6. What fallacies are given in the second class?

   Para. 52 – 75: ______

7. What is the ending of this story?

   Para. 76 – 104: ______

III. Learning the Language

◇ *Be aware of and sensitive to language variations and varieties.*

◇ *Choose the language as being used in the passage.*

◇ *Learn the best language.*

1. Take, ________ example, Petey Burch, my roommate at the University of Minnesota. Same age, same background, but dumb as an ox.
   A) as an B) for an C) as D) for
2. (He is an) emotional type. Unstable. Impressionable. ________ of all, a faddist.
   A) Best B) First C) Worst D) Most
3. Fads, I ________, are the very negation of reason.
   A) agree B) submit C) accept D) take
4. To be swept up in every new craze that comes along, to ________ yourself to idiocy just because everybody else is doing it—this, to me, is the greatest of mindlessness.
   A) surrender B) render C) agenda D) gender
5. I was well aware of the importance of the right kind of wife in ________ a lawyer's career. (Para. 1)
   A) furthering B) going on C) continuing D) developing
6. I had my first date with Polly the following evening. This was in nature of a(n) ________. (Para. 27)
   A) investigation B) survey C) research D) examination
7. I went back to my room with a heavy heart. I had gravely underestimated the ________ of my task. (Para. 28)
   A) dimension B) amount C) size D) range
8. I fought off a wave of despair. I was getting ________ with this girl, absolutely nowhere. Still, I am nothing if not persistent. (Para. 43)
   A) nowhere B) no place C) no space D) no result
9. Polly, I said sharply, it's a fallacy. Eula Becker doesn't cause the rain. She has no connection with the rain. You are ________ Post Hoc if you blame Eula Becker. (Para. 46)

A) erroneous of B) guilt of C) wrong of D) faulty of

10. My dear, I said, ________ her with a smile, we have spent five evenings together. We have gotten along splendid. It is clear that we are well matched. (Para. 78)

  A) satisfying B) pleasing C) favoring D) greeting

IV. Thinking Openly

◇ *Keep your mind open to new ideas.*

◇ *Be receptive to other's opinions.*

◇ *Challenge your own judgment.*

1. To be swept up in every new craze that comes along, to surrender yourself to idiocy just because everybody else is doing it—this, to me, is the greatest of mindlessness. Do you agree? (introduction)

____

____

2. It is, after all, easier to make a beautiful dumb girl smart than to make an ugly smart girl beautiful. Do you think the same way? (Para. 4)

____

____

3. Logic is the science of thinking. How much do you know about this science?

____

____

4. What is the fallacy of Dicto Simpliciter. ? Have you ever committed a fallacy of this kind? (Para. 33 – 36)

____

____

5. What is the fallacy of Hasty Generalization? Have you eve committed a fallacy of this kind? (Para. 39 – 41)

____

____

6. What is the fallacy of Post Hoc? Have you ever committed a fallacy of this kind? (Para. 44 – 46)

___

___

7. What is the fallacy of Ad Misericordiam? Have you ever committed a fallacy of this kind? (Para. 52 – 55)

___

___

8. What is the fallacy of False Analogy? Have you ever committed a fallacy of this kind? (Para. 58 – 61)

___

___

9. What is the fallacy of Hypothesis of Contrary to Fact? Have you ever committed a fallacy of this kind? (Para. 62 – 67)

___

___

10. What is the fallacy of Poisoning the Well? Have you ever committed a fallacy of this kind? (Para. 68 – 74)

___

___

V. Thinking Critically

◇ *Be critical in your thinking.*

◇ *Be skeptical in your thinking.*

◇ *Be introspective in your thinking.*

1. Have you ever had a girl/boy of pin-up proportions around you? What is her/him like?

___

___

2. Fads, I submit, are the very negation of reason. What do you think?

___

___

3. The successful lawyers I had observed were, almost without exceptions, married to beautiful, gracious, intelligent women. What ' s your comment on these three considerations in choosing a girl friend?

____

____

4. What is your comment on "Love is a fallacy."?

____

____

5. What kind of person is the narrator, the law school student?

____

____

6. What kind of person is Polly Espy, the girl in the same university?

____

____

7. What kind of person is Petey Burch, another law school student?

____

____

VI. Thinking Independently

◇ *Develop and form ideas or opinions of your own.*

◇ *Be both inductive and deductive in your thinking.*

◇ *Communicate and share with others.*

◇ *Write and present your composition on one of the following topics.*

1. A beautiful love story I have ever heard of
2. Love is a fallacy.
3. What do I expect from love?
4. To love is to give.
5. My choice between to love and to be loved
6. One thing I have learned from this passage

Passage 16

OF STUDIES

1 Studies serve for delight, for ornament, and for ability. Their chief use for delight, is in privateness and retirement; for ornament, is in discourse [serious conversation]; and for ability, is in judgment and disposition [settlement] of business.

2 Expert men are capable of executing and perhaps making judgment of the particulars one by one, but the general counseling [giving advice], and the planning and organizing of affairs, come best from those that are learned.

3 To spend too much time in studies is sluggish; to use them too much for ornament is self-affectionate; to make judgment wholly by rules from books is the humor [funny quality] of a scholar.

4 Studies perfect human nature and are perfected by experience-for, like natural plants, natural abilities need trimming by study. Studies themselves do give directions which are too much at large, unless they are bounded in by experience.

5 Crafty men contemn studies, simple men admire them, and wise men use them, for what they teach are not their own use, but wisdom beyond them and above them, which is acquired only by observation.

6 Read not to contradict and confute, nor to believe and take for

granted, nor to find talk and discourse, but to weigh and consider.

7 Some books are to be tasted, others to be swallowed, and some few to be chewed and digested; that is, some books are to be read only in parts, others to be browsed, and some few to be read wholly with diligence and attention. Some books also may be read by deputy [others], and just to read the extracts made of them will be enough; but this reading applies only to those books with less important arguments and those of meaner sort, otherwise extracted books, not much different from distilled [purified] waters, become tedious and tasteless things.

8 Reading makes a full man, conference [discussion] a witty man, and writing an exact man. Therefore, if a man write little, he had need of a great memory; if he confer [discuss] little, he had need of a present wit; and if he read little, he had need of much cunning, so as to seem to know that he does not.

9 Histories make men wise; poets, witty; the mathematics, subtle; natural philosophy, deep; moral philosophy, grave; logic and rhetoric, able to contend.

10 There is no stand or impairment in the mind that can not be worked out by suitable studies; like diseases of the body, that may have appropriate exercises. Bowling is good for the stone and reins [the kidneys]; shooting for the lungs and breast; gentle walking for the stomach; riding for the head; and the like.

11 So if a man's mind be wandering, let him study the mathematics; for in demonstrations, if his wit be called away a little, he must begin again. If his wit be not apt to distinguish or find differences, let him study the Schoolmen [medieval scholars], for they are analytic men. If he be not apt to beat over matters, and to call up one thing to prove and illustrate another, let him study the lawyers' cases. So every defect of the mind may have a special receipt.

WORDS AND PHRASES

bound *n.*	impose limit on
browse【brauz】*v.*	look through casually
confute *v.*	prove wrong
deputy *n.*	somebody fully appointed to act on behalf of somebody else
discourse【ˈdiskɔːs】*n.*	serious discussion or conversation
distill *v.*	purify liquid with heat
execute【ˈeksikjuːt】*v.*	perform action
receipt *n.*	recipe
reins【reinz】*n.*	the kidneys

I. Understanding the Text

论读书

读书给人以乐趣，给人以装点，给人以才干。此乐趣，常在独处悠闲之时；此装点，常现纵谈阔论之中；此才干，常见论辨决断之际。

专业之才固然实用能干，分析判断，循序渐进；但要论运筹帷幄，组织策划，则非博学饱读之士莫属。

读书耗时过多易惰，词藻太过华丽则矫，全凭书本条文论断事物乃可掬学究之故态。

读书可补先天之不足，经验又可补读书之不足；先天才能有如自然花草，须用读书加以修整；读书确能给人以方向引领，但唯有用经验加以确定，才可免于空泛。

身怀技艺者轻视读书，头脑缺欠者推崇读书，唯聪慧者善用读书。书，并不以用处告人，而以智慧示人；用书之智不在书中，而在书外，唯用心体察，方可得之。

读书不为驳辨，不可读而纳之，不可读而论之，而应细致权衡，用心思之。

书，有供欣赏者，有供浏览者，有供咀嚼消化者。换言之，有的书只需选读，有的只可略读，有的则须孜孜不倦用心通读。书，还可请人代读，取其所作摘要读之；如此书籍仅限少有观点或品位不高之类，否则，摘录的书如同蒸馏的水，索然而乏味。

读书使人充实，讨论使人机智，笔记使人准确。因此，不常作笔记者须有绝佳记忆，不常讨论者须有天生聪慧，不常读书者须变通有术，始能无知而显有知。

读史使人睿智，读诗使人灵秀，数学使人缜密，科学使人深刻，伦理学使人厚重，逻辑修辞学使人善辩；凡书中所学，皆成性格。

凡头脑滞碍，无不可以通过读适当的书加以排除；一如人体疾患，皆可借助适宜运动加以调治。滚球利肾脏，射箭阔胸肺，慢步养肠胃，骑术健头脑，诸如此类。

注意力不够专注，可让其学数学，演算求证需精力集中，稍有分神，则须推倒重来；辨析力欠缺，可让其读经院哲学，该派学者多为条分缕析之人；不善了断事务，难知彼而推此，可让其读律师的案卷。凡此头脑不足，皆有良方可求。

II. Thinking Critically

◇ *Be critical in your thinking.*

◇ *Be skeptical in your thinking.*

◇ *Be introspective in your thinking.*

1. Studies serve for delight, for ornament, and for ability. Do you agree? What books do you read for delight? (Para. 1)

____

____

2. Crafty men contemn studies, simple men admire them, and wise men use them. What do you think of the above statement? (Para. 5)

____

____

3. Read not to contradict and confute, nor to believe and take for granted, nor to find talk and discourse, but to weigh and consider. Do you agree with the statement? (Para. 6)

____

____

4. Reading makes a full man, conference [discussion] a witty man, and writing an exact man. What's your comment on the above statement? (Para. 8)

____

____

5. Histories make men wise; poets, witty; the mathematics, subtle; natural philosophy, deep; moral philosophy, grave; logic and rhetoric, able to contend. Do you agree? What books are your preference? (Para. 9)

____

____

6. So every defect of the mind may have a special receipt. What do you think? What receipt do you need? (Para. 11)

____

____

III. Thinking Independently

◇ *Develop and form ideas or opinions of your own.*

◇ *Be both inductive and deductive in your thinking.*

◇ *Communicate and share with others.*

◇ *Write and present your composition on one of the following topics.*

1. Of Reading
2. What reading means to me.
3. Reading is part of my life.
4. The kind of book that I like to read
5. One thin that I do not agree with the writer
6. One thing I have learned from this passage

Glossary

A

a host of	a large number of (2)
a straight "A" student	one who has the highest grade in all courses (7)
abridge *v.*	restrict one's rights (12)
acute【ə'kjut】*adj.*	perceptive and intelligent (15)
adrift【ə'drift】*adj.*	floating (12)
adversity【əd'və:səti】*n.*	misfortune; misery (11)
affirmative *n.*	positive assertion (3)
affront【ə'frʌnt】*v.*	insult openly (7)
algebra【'ældʒibrə】*n.*	代数 (7)
amass *v.*	accumulate, collect (14)
analogy【ə'nælədʒi】*n.*	the reasoning or explanation given by comparing similar points (15)
annuity【ə'nju:əti】*n.*	annual income (13)
arbitrary【a:bitrəri】*adj.*	based on one's own wishes or will (12)
articulately *adv.*	spoken or expressed clearly (9)
assertion【ə'səʃən】*n.*	definite statement (4)
at one's command	ready to be used (2)
attain【ə'tein】*v.*	gain esp. after long effort (13)
attribute【'ætribju:t】*n.*	quality; characteristic (4)
authentically【ɔ:θentikli】*adv.*	sincerely (11)

B

backfire【'bækfaiə】*v.*	have the opposite result (6)
bear out	show to be right; confirm (7)
bearing *n.*	way of moving or standing (15)
befall【bi'fɔ:l】*v.*	happen (5)
beneficent【bi'nefisənt】*adj.*	doing good (7)
binding【'baindiŋ】*adv.*	having power to hold one to an agreement (9)
blush *v.*	become red in face (15)
bound *n.*	impose limit on (16)
breeding *n.*	upbringing, education and training in one's manners (15)
brink【briŋk】*n.*	verge; edge (5)
brow *n.*	forehead (15)
browse【brauz】*v.*	look through casually (16)

C

carriage *n.*	way of holding the body (15)
case history	a record of someone suffering from an illness or social difficulties (7)
catch phrase	a phrase that catches attention (5)
categorize【'kætəgəraiz】*v.*	put into groups (6)
celestially【si'lestjəli】*adv.*	as in heaven (4)
censure【'senʃə】*n.*	rebuke (12)
channel *v.*	guide/send through a channel (11)
chuckle *v.*	laugh quietly (15)
circumference【sə'kʌmfərəns】*n.*	the boundary line of a circle (7)
clamber【'klæmbə】*v.*	climb with difficulty (12)

clap *v.*	applaud (15)
cluster【ˈklʌstə】*n.*	a number of (12)
compartmentalize【kəmpaːtˈmentəlaiz】*v.*	divide things into separate parts (9)
compassion【kəmˈpæʃən】*n.*	pity; sympathy (5)
compassionate【kəmˈpæʃənit】*adj.*	sympathetic (11)
compatibility【kəmˌpætəˈbiləti】*n.*	the ability to exist or live/work with sb. else (9)
complexion【kəmˈplekʃən】*n.*	color of skin (12)
composition *n.*	constituent; makeup (3)
conceive of	consider; think of (7)
confess *v.*	admit openly a wrongdoing (16)
confidant【ˈkɔnfidænt】*n.*	a person trusted (9)
conformity【kənˈfɔːməti】*n.*	behavior that follows accepted rules (1)
confute *v.*	prove wrong (16)
congeniality【kənˌdʒiːniˈæliti】*n.*	the same or similar nature (9)
constellation【kɔnstəˈleiʃən】*n.*	a group of stars (15)
contemplate【ˈkɔntempleit】*v.*	look at thoughtfully for a long time (8)
contrapuntal【ˌkɔntrəˈpʌntl】*adj.*	relating to/marked by counterpoint (9)
control class	(做实验)对照班 (2)
correlative【kəˈrelətiv】*adj.*	naturally related (3)
cowpox【ˈkaupɔks】*n.*	牛痘 (10)
croak【krəuk】*v.*	sound of a frog or crow (15)
cross-section	a representative example of the whole (2)
crutch【krʌtʃ】*n.*	a support to help a lame person to walk (7)

D

demagogue【'deməgɔg】*n.*	person influencing the common people by speeches (4)
deputy *n.*	somebody fully appointed to act on behalf of somebody else (16)
detach *n.*	not attach; separate (8)
devoid *adj.*	empty of; lacking in something (14)
diabolically【daiə'bɔlikəli】*adv.*	like a devil (4)
disciple【di'saipl】*n.*	believer in or follower of a thought or teaching (12)
discourse【'diskɔ:s】*n.*	serious discussion or conversation (16)
distill *v.*	purify liquid with heat (16)
distort *v.*	five inaccurate report (3)
dogmatic【dɔg'mætik】*adj.*	making assertions (4)
down to the last detail	in every detail (7)
draw out	cause to come out (9)
draw upon	make use of (9)
drudgery【'dʒʌdʒəri】*n.*	hard and uninteresting work (8)
dumb【dʌm】*adj.*	slow in understanding, stupid (7)
dump in sb's lap	make a lucky event come to a person with no effort of his own (7)
duo【'dju:əu】*n.*	two performers singing or playing together (13)
dynamo【'dainəmou】*n.*	generator of electricity (15)
dyslexia【dis'leksiə】*n.*	inability to read (13)

E

Easter Bunny	复活节的小兔子(礼物)(5)
egocentric【ˌigəusentrik】*adj.*	viewing everything in relation to oneself (5)
emancipation *n.*	act of freeing (3)
emphatic【imˈfætik】*adj.*	of emphasis (13)
enchantment【inˈtʃa:ntmənt】*n.*	great delight (12)
enlightenment【inˈlaitənmənt】*n.*	a true understanding of things (4)
enthrall【inˈθrɔ:l】*v.*	captivate (5)
erase【iˈreiz】*v.*	rub/scrape out (10)
execute【ˈeksikju:t】*v.*	perform action (16)
exquisite【ˈekskwizit】*adj.*	delicate; very fine (15)

F

fad【fæd】*n.*	a fashion that lasts for a short time (15)
Fair (pun)	referring to women (12)
familial【fəˈmiljəl】*adj.*	relating to the family (4)
flank【flæŋk】*v.*	attack the side (10)
flashy【ˈflæʃi】*adj.*	giving a momentary impression; showy (5)
formulation【ˌfɔ:mjuˈleiʃən】*n.*	the way of defining a problem (14)
fraction【ˈfrækʃən】*n.*	a small part (2)
frantic【ˈfræntik】*adj.*	wildly excited (4)
fraudulency【ˈfrɔ:djulənsi】*n.*	deception (14)

G

gadget['gædʒit] *n.*	a small device (14)
gallant['gælənt] *adj.*	brave (5)
goad[goud] *v.*	stir up; incite (4)
going['gəuiŋ] *n.*	conditions for progress (10)
gurgle *v.*	make a bubbling sound of water (15)

H

hang-dog *adj.*	ashamed; guilty (7)
haphazard[hæp'hæzəd] *adj.*	not planned (2)
hard-headed *adj.*	shrewd and unsentimental (2)
head-on *adv.*	in a direct manner (10)
heed[hi:d] *v.*	pay serious attention to (13)
heretofore [ˌhiətu:'fɔ] *adv.*	until now (7)
hierarchy[haiəra:ki] *n.*	formally ranked group (8)
honorable mention	an honorary award next below those that win prizes (7)
humiliation[hju:ˌmili'eiʃən] *n.*	disgrace; shame (7)

I

identical[ai'dentikəl] *adj.*	exactly equal/alike (2)
idiocy['idiəsi] *n.*	great foolishness; of an idiot (15)
imbecility[imbə'siliti] *n.*	great stupidity (4)
impasse['impæs] *n.*	a position from which progress is impossible(10)
impetus['impitəs] *n.*	a driving force (11)
in one's own right	through one's own authority or ability(11)

in the swim	familiar with the current tendencies (15)
in the throes of	struggling with(12)
incidentally *adv.*	by the way (3)
indignation *n.*	anger with scorn(15)
induce *v.*	persuade somebody to do sth. (3)
infuse【ˈinfjuːs】*v.*	introduce something into somebody's mind (14)
ingredient *n.*	element required for something (8)
inherit【inˈherit】*v.*	receive property from someone after they die(1)
instinct【ˈinstiŋkt】*n.*	a natural feeling, knowledge, or power (1)
interminable【inˈtəːminəbl】*adj.*	endless (12)
intoxicant【inˈtɔksikənt】*n.*	something which makes one lose control of oneself (4)
irreconcilable【iˌrekənˈsailəbl】*adj.*	impossible to find agreement with (9)

J

justifiable【ˌdʒʌstiˈfaiəbl】*adj.*	be justified (6)

L

lamely *adv.*	unconvincingly(12)
lament【ləˈment】*v.*	regret deeply (11)
languish *v.*	be neglected (15)
lash【læʃ】*n.*	an eyelash (15)
lateral【ˈlætərəl】*adj.*	of/at the side (1)
leave off	stop doing something (9)

liar【laiə】*n.*	a person telling a lie (6)
liquidate【ˈlikwideit】*v.*	get rid of (4)

M

make oneself at home	be comfortable with one's surroundings (1)
manipulate【məˈnipjuleit】*v.*	handle with skill (11)
mansion【ˈmænʃən】*n.*	a very large house (1)
maneuver【məˈnu:və】*n.*	a skillful move/trick (10)
mediocrity【ˌmi:diˈɔkrəti】*n.*	the state of being neither good nor bad (2)
miraculous *adj.*	extraordinary and marvelous (7)
mole【məul】*n.*	痣(12)
muster【ˈmʌstə】*n.*	come up to the required standard (12)

N

norm【nɔ:m】*n.*	standard; model (13)

O

obsess【əbˈses】*v.*	preoccupy (14)
omission【əˈmiʃən】*n.*	something omitted (6)
option【ˈɔpʃən】*n.*	choice (11)
orator【ˈɔrətə】*n.*	a person skilled in public speaking (2)
orthodox【ˈɔ:θədɔks】*adj.*	holding the accepted beliefs (11)
overtone【ˈəuvətəun】*n.*	a hint or suggestion (12)
out of step	not move or agree at the same rate (9)

P

parable【ˈpærəbl】*n.*	a brief story to teach some moral lesson/truth (10)
paradoxical【ˌpærəˈdɔksikəl】*adj.*	self-contradictory (12)
parody【ˈpærədi】*n.*	a humorous imitation (5)
pathetic【pəˈθetik】*adj.*	causing a feeling of pity or sorrow (6)
pedagogical【ˌpedəˈgɔdʒikl】*adj.*	of science or art of teaching (12)
perspicacious【pəːspiˈkeiʃəs】*adj.*	far-seeing; having good judgment (15)
photographic *adj.*	of photography (15)
pin-up *n.*	a picture pinned on a wall (15)
pitchblende【ˈpitʃblend】*n.*	沥青铀 (15)
ply【plai】*v.*	to use diligently as a tool/weapon (13)
poise *n.*	calm self-assured dignity (15)
post-Christian (countries)	dragged behind in believing in Christianity (12)
preen【priːn】*v.*	dress with elaborate care (12)
premise【ˈpremis】*n.*	a statement assumed to be true or used to draw conclusion (7)
premium【ˈpriːmjəm】*n.*	prize or reward (14)
prevail upon	persuade (7)
profound【prəˈfaund】*adj.*	very deep (6)
prolific【prəˈlifik】*adj.*	productive (13)
prone【prəun】*adj.*	be subject to (13)
prop up	hold up by placing a support (12)
prosecution *n.*	the act of carrying out an activity or occupation (14)
prudential【pruˈdenʃəl】*adj.*	exercising good judgment or common sense (13)

pshaw【ʃɔ:】*n.* expressing disbelief, impatience, or contempt (15)

put the cart before the horse do things in the wrong order (2)

Q

quadruple【'kwɔdrupl】*v.* increase by four times (2)

R

raccoon【ræku:n】*n.* 浣熊大衣 (15)

rationalization【ˌræʃənəli'zeiʃən】*n.* the process of rationalizing (14)

receipt *n.* recipe (16)

reins【reinz】*n.* the kidneys (16)

Renaissance【ri'neisəns】*n.* 文艺复兴 (13)

renounce【ri'nauns】*v.* declare to give up (12)

repress【ri'pres】*v.* beat down; suppress (11)

rigid【'ridʒid】*adj.* stiff; firm (11)

rung【rʌŋ】*n.* a bar forming a step of a ladder (13)

S

s. o. b. (Am sl.) son of a bitch (5)

sanity【'sænəti】*n.* the state of having a healthy mind (7)

scalpel【'skælpəl】*n.* a surgeon's sharp knife used in operations (15)

scourge【skə:dʒ】*n.* thing or person that causes great trouble/misfortune (10)

Second the second sex (women) (12)

sergeant【'sa:dʒənt】*n.* an officer in the army (6)

shambling【'ʃæmbliŋ】*n*.	walking in a lazy or clumsy manner (15)
shriek【ʃriːk】*v*.	give a sharp cry (15)
shrug *n*.	gesture of raising or dropping the shoulders (15)
slack【slæk】*adj*.	loose; not tight (10)
slapstick【'slæpstik】*n*.	a paddle designed to produce a loud sound (13)
slovenly【slʌvənli】*adj*.	careless about one's personal hygiene and tidiness (14)
smallpox【'smɔːlpɔks】*n*.	a contagious disease causing spots on the skin (10)
smash【smæʃ】*n*.	a hit; a success (13)
sobriety【sou'braiəti】*n*.	ability to judge things calmly (4)
spectacular【spek'tækjulə】*adj*.	very grand (13)
spontaneous【spɔn'teinjəs】*adj*.	self-starting (11)
stagger *v*.	move unsteadily, nearly falling (15)
status quo	<拉>现状 (11)
stay put	stay in place (9)
stereotype【'steriətaip】*v*.	have a fixed pattern (6)
stick one's head in the sand	pay little or no attention (5)
stifling【'staifliŋ】*adj*.	oppressive; allowing no room for free thought or action (4)
strain【strein】*n*.	too much effort (7)
streak【striːk】*n*.	a slight tendency, esp. in contrast with one's general character (11)
strike up	start to play or sing (9)
stunt *n*.	dangerous feat (8)
subdue【səb'djuː】*v*.	overcome, conquer (14)
succinctly【sək'siŋktli】*adv*.	concisely (14)

T

temperament【ˈtemprəmənt】*n.*	a person's nature (9)
tentatively【ˈtentətivli】*adv.*	by way of a test (9)
the breath of life	the most important thing in one's life (9)
transaction【trænˈzækʃən】*n.*	a deal in business (6)
transpose【trænsˈpəuz】*v.*	reverse the order or place of (13)
traumatic【trɔːmætik】*adj.*	startling; shocking (11)
turn a blind eye (to)	pay no attention to (6)

U

ulterior【ʌlˈtiəriə】*n.*	lying outside (14)
upstairs (AmE slang)	empty minded (15)

V

vaccination【ˌvæksiˈneiʃən】*n.*	接种疫苗 (10)
verify【ˈverifai】*v.*	prove to be true (7)
vestige【ˈvestidʒ】*n.*	trace of something gone (12)
vulnerable【ˈvʌlnərəbl】*adj.*	that can be wounded or injured(5)

W

wag *v.*	move something to and fro (15)
wcll-primed *adj.*	filled; prepared (4)
woebegone【ˈwəubigɔn】*adj.*	looking sad or sorrowful or wretched(7)

Z

Zen【zen;zɛn】*n.* emphasizing the value of meditation and intuition (10)

zest【zest】*n.* enthusiasm (11)

Catch Phrase List

Passage 1

1. On average, people only use 1% of their brain power in everyday life. It is as though we have inherited a huge mansion and decided to live in the bathroom. (Para. 3)
2. Different parts of the brain control different areas of our thinking process. The left side of the brain controls logic and learning. The right side controls our imagination and our artistic sense. (Para. 7)
3. If we are given a choice between two things that work equally well we will always choose the most beautiful. This fact shows the influence of our right brain. (Para. 9)
4. At every level, the future belongs to those who can dream. (Para. 10)

Passage 2

5. If your vocabulary is limited your chances of success are limited. (Para. 2)
6. The extent of your vocabulary indicates the degree of your intelligence. (Para. 7)
7. Words are your tools of thought. (Para. 10)
8. And the more words you have at your command, the deeper, clearer and more accurate will be your thinking. (Para. 11)
9. Your words are your personality. Your vocabulary is you. (Para. 12)
10. Words are explosive. Phrases are packed with TNT. (Para. 14)
11. Words can also change the direction of your life. They have often raised a man from mediocrity to success. (Para. 15)

Passage 3

12. It is by no means uncommon to find men whose knowledge is wide but whose feelings are narrow. Such men lack what I am calling wisdom. (Para. 3)
13. Even an end which it would be noble to pursue may be pursued unwisely. (Para. 4)
14. With every increase of knowledge and skill, wisdom becomes more necessary. (Para. 7)

Passage 4

15. Reading is a private, not a collective activity. (Para. 2)
16. Unlike the masses, intellectuals have a taste for rationality and an interest in facts. (Para. 3)
17. Philosophy teaches us to feel uncertain about the things that seem to us self-evident. (Para. 4)

Passage 5

18. The road from realization to acceptance is a lot longer than it looks. (Para. 7)
19. The past is the past. (Para. 7)
20. Saying and doing are two different things. (Para. 7)
21. Second chances are few, and it's much easier to do it right the first time. (Para. 7)
22. The tables have turned. (Para. 10)

Passage 6

23. In a society where lying is common, trust becomes impossible, and without trust, cooperation cannot exist. (Para. 2)
24. One person's "little white lie" is another person's "dirty lie." (Para. 8)

25. We shouldn't be too hard on ourselves, but if we have turned a blind eye to our faults, we should take an honest look in the mirror. (Para. 12)

Passage 7

26. This self-image becomes a golden key to living a better life. (Para. 2)
27. The self-image is a "premise," a base, or a foundation upon which your entire personality, your behavior, and even your circumstances are built. (Para. 3)
28. Jesus warned us about the folly of putting a patch of new material upon an old garment, or of putting new wine into old bottles. (Para. 8)
29. In fact, it is literally impossible to really think positively about a particular situation, as long as you hold a negative concept of self. (Para. 8)

Passage 8

30. Except to people with unusual initiative it is positively agreeable to be told what to do. (Para. 2)
31. Work therefore is desirable, first and foremost, as a preventive of boredom. (Para. 3)
32. Continuity of purpose is one of the most essential ingredients of happiness in the long run. (Para. 4)
33. Two chief elements make work interesting; first, the exercise of skill, and second, construction. (Para. 5)
34. Those who find satisfaction in construction find in it greater satisfaction than the lovers of destruction can find in destruction. (Para. 7)
35. Few things are likely to cure the habit of hatred. But nothing can rob a man of the happiness of successful achievement in an important piece of work. (Para. 7)

36. Without self-respect genuine happiness is scarcely possible. And the man who is ashamed of his work can hardly achieve self-respect. (Para. 9)
37. The habit of viewing life as a whole is an essential part both of wisdom and of true morality, and is one of the things which ought to be encouraged in education. (Para. 10)
38. Consistent purpose is not enough to make life happy, but it is an almost indispensable condition of a happy life. And consistent purpose embodies itself mainly in work. (Para. 10)

Passage 9

39. There is the recognition that friendship, in contrast with kinship, invokes freedom of choice. A friend is someone who chooses and is chosen. (Para. 11)
40. And between friends there is inevitably a kind of equality of give-and-take. (Para. 11)

Passage 10

41. "When the going gets tough, the tough gets going," is typical of this aggressive attitude toward problem-solving. (Para. 6)
42. Looking at a crisis from an opportunity point of view is a lateral thought. (Para. 14)

Passage 11

43. Few people are one hundred percent winners or one hundred percent losers. It's a matter of degree. (Para. 3)
44. However, once a person is on the road to being a winner, his chances are greater for becoming even more so. (Para. 3)
45. He (a winner) can separate facts from opinion and doesn't pretend to have all the answers. (Para. 5)
46. He (a winner) can discipline himself in the present to enhance his

enjoyment in the future. (Para. 7)

47. Winners successfully make the transition from total helplessness to independence, and then to interdependence. (Para. 9)
48. Few people are total winners or losers. Most of them are winners in some areas of their lives and losers in others. (Para. 10)
49. A loser has difficulty giving and receiving affection. He dose not enter into intimate, honest direct relationships with others. (Para. 13)
50. Integration helps a person make the transition from dependency to self-sufficiency. (Para. 18)

Passage 12

51. The privileges of beauty are immense. To be sure, beauty is a form of power. And deservedly so. (Para. 8)
52. Beauty is not the power to do but the power to attract. It is a power that negates itself. For this power is not one that can be chosen freely—at least, not by women. (Para. 8)

Passage 13

53. For every strength you have, you also possess a multitude of non-strengths. (Para. 3)
54. Everyone needs support of some sort. It can be as simple as eyeglasses to correct poor vision. (Para. 15)

Passage 14

55. In the process of work, that is, the molding and changing of nature outside of himself, man molds and changes himself. (Para. 1)
56. The more it was possible to gain riches by work, the more it became a pure means to the aim of wealth and success. (Para. 3)

Passage 15

57. Fads are the very negation of reason.

Passage 16

58. Crafty men contemn studies, simple men admire them, and wise men use them. (Para. 5)
59. Reading makes a full man, conference [discussion] a witty man, and writing an exact man. (Para. 8)
60. Histories make men wise; poets, witty; the mathematics, subtle; natural philosophy, deep; moral philosophy, grave; logic and rhetoric, able to contend. (Para. 9)